LT
SF

D1221136

LONE STAR RIDER

Center Point
Large Print

**This Large Print Book carries the
Seal of Approval of N.A.V.H.**

LONE STAR RIDER

Bradford Scott

CENTER POINT LARGE PRINT
THORNDIKE, MAINE

This Center Point Large Print edition
is published in the year 2016 by arrangement with
Golden West Literary Agency.

First US edition: Pyramid Books

The text of this Large Print edition is unabridged.
In other aspects, this book may vary
from the original edition.
Printed in the United States of America
on permanent paper.
Set in 16-point Times New Roman type.

ISBN: 978-1-62899-945-7 (hardcover)
ISBN: 978-1-62899-949-5 (paperback)

Library of Congress Cataloging-in-Publication Data

Names: Scott, Bradford, 1893–1975, author.
Title: Lone star rider / Bradford Scott.
Description: Center Point Large Print edition. | Thorndike, Maine :
Center Point Large Print, 2016. | ©1960
Identifiers: LCCN 2016001524| ISBN 9781628999457 (hardcover : alk.
paper) | ISBN 9781628999495 (paperback : alk. paper)
Subjects: LCSH: Large type books. | GSAFD: Western stories.
Classification: LCC PS3537.C9265 L647 2016 | DDC 813/.52—dc23
LC record available at http://lccn.loc.gov/2016001524

ONE

"Well, Doc, I think I'll have another cup of coffee, finish my cigarette, and then hit the trail. Shadow is rested and it'll be cooler riding during the night hours."

"Not figuring on doing the sixty miles to Cholla in one night, are you?" asked Doc Cooper.

Ranger Walt Slade, whom the Mexicans of the Rio Grande river villages named *El Halcon*—The Hawk—smiled and shook his head.

"Nope, I'm not riding a race," he replied. "Along about daylight I'll curl up in some shady grove or thicket, sleep a few hours and make Cholla sometime in the afternoon, if nothing happens."

"Something's always happening in that blasted Border town, or in the hills around it," grunted the old frontier practitioner. "Uh-huh, something bad."

Slade chuckled. "Appears plenty of that sort has already happened of late," he replied.

"Gather there has, or you wouldn't be headed in that direction," commented Cooper. "I'm moving down there soon myself, where business for a doctor is booming, though the undertaker is the real bully boy with a glass eye there. Here's the coffee, steaming hot."

5

As Slade sipped the coffee, Doc Cooper thought what a splendid-looking man he was, his lean, deeply bronzed high-nosed face dominated by long, black-lashed eyes of pale gray. They were gay, reckless eyes that despite their coldness always seemed to have little dancing devils of laughter in their depths. Doc knew those eyes could subtly change color at times, seemingly growing paler and with the devils of laughter replaced by devils of a very different nature. Above the broad forehead was thick, crisp hair so black a blue shadow seemed to lie upon it. The mouth below the hawk nose was rather wide, with a grin-quirking at the corners that relieved somewhat the sternness, almost fierceness, evinced by the high-bridged nose, the powerful chin and jaw and the cold eyes.

Eyes that can grin at you one minute and look sudden death and destruction at you back of a gunsight the next, Doc thought.

Nor did Slade's form belie his face. More than six feet tall, the breadth of his shoulders and the depth of his chest matched his height.

Slade wore the plain and efficient garb of the rangeland with careless grace—bibless overalls, faded blue shirt, vivid handkerchief looped, cowboy style, about his throat, high-heeled half-boots of softly tanned leather, and a battered, broad-brimmed "J.B." Double cartridge belts encircled his lean waist and the plain black butts of heavy, long-barreled Colts showed above the carefully worked and oiled cut-out holsters.

Finishing his coffee, Slade rolled a cigarette with the slim fingers of his left hand. He could do anything with those slender hands, even to keeping them perfectly still.

El Halcon smoked in silence, and with evident enjoyment. Abruptly he pinched out the butt and stood up, smiling down at the old doctor from his great height. "Be seeing you," he said, and strode out the door, closing it softly behind him.

From around the corner came the hum of Harding's night life, but Doc Cooper's office was on a quiet side street and off the railroad town's main thoroughfare. Nobody was in sight as Slade gathered up the split reins that trailed the ground—all Shadow needed to keep him securely "tied"—and swung into the saddle. The tall horse was black as the night itself and his dainty hoofs made almost no sound as he moved forward with a lithe grace that was muscular perfection.

Slade rode south by west, following the old Apache Trail that wound through the distant Cholla Hills to finally reach the Mexican Border, cross the Rio Grande and continue into the mountains of the land of *mañana*.

It was a windy night, with hurrying patches of cloud obscuring the moonlight from time to time, so that Slade rode a checkerboard of alternating black and silver. However, he did not think it was going to rain and enjoyed the coolness after a hot and sultry day.

He had covered about five miles when from the darkness ahead came a distance-thinned crackling, like to thorns burning briskly under a pot. Slade straightened in the saddle and became alert.

"Sure sounded like shooting," he remarked to Shadow. "Now what in blazes?"

Silence followed the spasm of reports, silence that endured for a few minutes and was broken by a single echoless clap that held an oddly muffled note.

"Like some loco jigger held the muzzle of his shootin' iron against the ground and pulled the trigger," Slade muttered.

The wind-ruffled stillness of the night closed down again. Slade rode on, still very much on the alert. Of course what he had heard could be a bunch of skylarking cowhands headed for town and a bust, but it could be something less innocent; the Apache Trail between Harding and Cholla was a track with a sinister history and a present that was little less dubious than the past.

No more reports quivered the air, but gradually another sound burred the sharp edge of the silence, at first a faint whisper. Swiftly it loudened to a soft mutter, deepened to a steady drumming, became a rhythmic pound that could only be the beat of speeding horses' hoofs churning the dust of the trail. Slade slowed Shadow's gait and glanced about.

A heavy bank of cloud was crossing the moon and the gloom was close to total darkness. He could just make out a straggle of thicket edging the trail. Into the edge of the growth he backed Shadow and pulled him to a halt.

"We'll try and get a look at those fast-riding gents without them seeing us," he told the black. "May be no reason to, but just the same we won't take any needless chances. That shooting sounded like some trigger-happy gents on the loose. We'll play it safe, horse."

Shadow blew softly through his nose to signify assent. Perfectly motionless, he was a solid block of darkness in the gloom. Slade also sat motionless, straining his eyes down the barely perceptible gray ribbon that was the trail. He was at the apex of a brush-flanked curve and his range of vision wound have been short even in daylight.

Louder and louder sounded the pounding hoofs. Now Slade could hear the creak and pop of saddle leather and the jingle of bridle irons. Another moment and his keen ears detected low voices. His black brows drew together. It was not the jolly conversation and laughter to be expected from carefree cowhands anticipating the pleasures of a night in town, but the muttering drone of men with serious matters to discuss who instinctively kept their voices down.

Around the bend to the south bulged a solider block of shadow, sweeping toward where the motionless Ranger sat his motionless horse. The band was less than fifty yards distant when the unexpected happened. The clouds broke apart like torn paper. Moonlight funneled down in a spout of silver radiance that seemed to center on where Slade sat his horse in the edge of the growth.

There was a startled exclamation, and a torrent of curses. Slade saw a gleam of shifted metal. Instantly, obedient to knee pressure, Shadow bounded convulsively to one side and went into a weaving dance. Slade swung far to the left as orange flame gushed from the ranks of the approaching horsemen and a slug sang by so close he felt the lethal breath of its passing. A second bullet whipped the sleeve of his shirt. Then El Halcon's guns let go with a rattling crash.

A scream of pain echoed the drumroll of reports, and a volley of answering shots. But Shadow, weaving and shifting, and Slade, swaying and ducking in unison with his mount's movements, were an elusive target against the ragged background of the brush. Another scream sounded as Slade pulled trigger, a scream that rose to a bubbling shriek and was chopped off short. Slade saw a rider whirl from his saddle and thud to the ground. The rest of the band, perhaps a dozen in number, swept past, shooting and cursing.

The hammers of Slade's Colts clicked on empty shells. He slammed them into their holsters and flipped his heavy Winchester from the saddle boot under his thigh. But before he could line the rifle, the band of night riders swept around the curve to the north and out of sight. His eyes never leaving the prone and motionless form in the dust of the trail, Slade listened intently to the fading pound of hoofs.

"Kept going, all right," he said to Shadow. "Take it easy, horse, and let's see what we bagged. I figure another hellion isn't feeling any too comfortable, either, from the way he yelled."

His attention still focused on the body, he dismounted and moved forward cautiously. If the devil was only wounded, he could be as dangerous as a broken-backed rattler.

But the man in the trail never moved, which Slade felt was not surprising when he saw that the slug which downed him had torn out one whole side of his throat. After glancing up the trail and listening for another moment, he knelt beside the dead man, who proved to be a hard-looking but scrubby specimen with nothing outstanding about him.

"Border scum!" Slade muttered. "Now what the devil is this all about?"

With deft fingers he searched the body, and found nothing of significance save a surprisingly large sum of money, which he replaced. Rocking back on his heels, he sat thinking hard for a moment. Then he straightened up and swung into the saddle.

"Hightail, horse," he said. "I've a notion we'd better sift sand in the direction of that shooting we heard. And I have a hunch we aren't going to like what we find."

He had covered something under two miles when ahead sounded a plaintive whinny, the call of a horse in distress. Tense and vigilant, Slade rode on, hoping that the clouds wouldn't bank up over the moon again. He slowed Shadow's gait as a brush-grown bend showed ahead, rounding the curve almost at a walk. The trail straightened out and he swore explosively.

Less than a score of yards distant was the clumsy bulk of a stagecoach, its front wheels cramped against the body, its front horses tangled in the harness. Both doors hung open. And sprawled in the dust were three motionless figures.

Slade sent Shadow forward. He swung to the ground with the black horse still in motion and approached the three bodies. A single glance told him that two were beyond human help; the bodies were riddled with buckshot and also bore several pistol wounds.

"Never had a chance," Slade muttered. "Dead before they hit the ground."

The third man, a lanky individual with grizzled hair, was still breathing, although he looked more dead than alive.

El Halcon knelt beside the man he rightly decided was the driver. The right side of his shirt was soaked with blood, his face was blackened by burned powder and there was a bullet wound almost over his left eye that had the appearance of being fatal. But a swift examination by Slade's sensitive fingers showed that the slug had glanced off the bone and had come out over the driver's left ear instead of going through his head. From the powder burns on his face, Slade concluded that the gun which inflicted the wound had been held almost against the man's head.

Working swiftly, he cut away the right arm of the blood soaked shirt. There was a hole through the top of the man's shoulder, from which blood was still seeping.

Slade strode to where Shadow stood with forward pricked, questioning ears. From his saddle pouch, he took a small jar of antiseptic salve and a roll of bandage, with which he padded and bound up the shoulder. The head wound was beyond him.

"Got to get him to the doctor fast," he told Shadow. "Maybe Cooper can pull him through, if there isn't a bad skull fracture. Just a minute, feller, and I'll be with you."

He stripped the stage horses of harness and turned them loose, knowing they could fend for themselves until picked up. Then he lifted the heavy body of the wounded man, apparently without effort, inserted a toe into a stirrup, straightened up carefully and swung into the saddle, cradling his burden against his broad breast.

"Let's go, horse," he ordered. "Fast but easy."

Shadow responded with a smooth running walk that ate up the miles and occasioned a minimum of jolting. Less than an hour had passed when Slade halted him in front of Doc Cooper's office in the dark and silent side street of Harding. On the way to town he had kept a sharp lookout for the murderous band which had ridden in the same direction, although he did not expect to overtake the killers. Very likely they had pulled onto a side trail, of which there were several, and had not approached the railroad town. Anyhow, Slade saw nothing of them.

Doc Cooper had gone to bed, but he responded quickly to Slade's knock.

"Well, I might have known it," he sputtered. "Can't you let an hour go by without shooting somebody? Bring him in. Who—blazes! It's Hank Givens, the Cholla-Harding stage driver! Put him on the table; you can tell me what happened later. I'll give him a heart stimulant first thing. Lost considerable blood and suffered severe shock. Ticker's still going, but none too strong. Then we'll give that hat rack a once-over. See you took care of the shoulder wound proper. A good surgeon was lost when you didn't decide to take up medicine in college instead of engineering. You've got the hands, and no nerves. Steady now, here's the needle. There, that should hold him. Now for the head."

The old doctor's examination was swift but thorough. "Concussion and a little fracture," was his diagnosis. "Yes, I think he'll pull through—tough as a pine knot—but he'd have been a goner if you hadn't gotten him here in a hurry. Help me to put him to bed and then tell me what happened. He'll get his senses back after he sleeps a while."

The injured driver was put to bed. Doc started coffee heating, stuffed a black pipe with blacker tobacco and glanced inquiringly at Slade.

The Ranger told him what he had experienced. "And that's all I know about it," he concluded.

"Those other two poor jiggers must have been the guards," Doc observed thoughtfully. "Always two of 'em when the stage is packing a gold shipment from the bank or one of the Cholla mines."

"Logical to think the stage was carrying a valuable shipment," Slade agreed. "I didn't have time to look things over carefully. Knew I must get the wounded man to you without delay."

"The right thing to do," agreed Cooper. "Chances are you wouldn't have learned much. The Cholla Raiders are darned efficient and don't leave any clues."

"The Cholla Raiders?"

"Uh-huh, a bunch that's been raising hell and shoving a chunk under a corner in this section

15

during recent months. If they got a gold shipment this time, it'll make the third. Been running off cows, too, and two weeks ago they hit the Ternoga Bank; got fifteen thousand in coin and bills. Hang out somewhere in the Cholla Hills and swoop down like hen hawks on a settin' quail. A bad bunch, with somebody who's got brains running them."

Slade nodded. It was because of the activities of the Cholla Raiders, although this was the first time he had heard them called by name, that he was in the section. For some moments he sat sipping coffee and smoking. Abruptly he stood up.

"Doc," he said, "when you are asked who brought Givens in, say it was a man in cowhand clothes who left right after he delivered Givens to you. I *am* leaving right away. Want to give that stage a once-over before somebody shows up there. You might mention that I said the bunch ran into me on the trail and threw some lead at me, and that I threw some back and downed one of them. That'll be enough. I think it best not to advertise the fact that I was mixed up in the affair. That could put certain gents on guard against me, which I prefer to avoid if possible. I'm hoping nobody down here knows of my Ranger connections. May make my chore easier."

"Think you'll be recognized as El Halcon, who, as folks say, 'if he isn't an owlhoot he misses being one by the skin of his teeth'?"

"Wouldn't be surprised," Slade replied cheerfully. "Lots of Mexicans hereabouts and plenty of them know me as El Halcon. Very likely I'll be recognized—as El Halcon; but that doesn't matter."

"Except that it makes you fair game for any trigger-itchy lawman, to say nothing of the outlaws and fast-draw gents out to get a reputation by downing the notorious El Halcon," Doc grunted. "Captain McNelty has told you that more than once."

"Yep," Slade replied, still cheerful, "but so far he hasn't forbidden me to work under cover, so I'll take a chance. Now give me an hour's start and then call in the town marshal and have him notify the sheriff at Cholla, where I understand he hangs out most of the time, of what happened. Wouldn't be surprised if the folks here at the stage station are already getting worried because their equipage hasn't shown up. Be seeing you, Doc. I think I'll make it to Cholla this time, only a bit later than I anticipated."

TWO

The dead outlaw lay in the same position when Slade passed; and there were no footprints around the body, which he considered fairly good evidence that nobody had ridden that way since the shooting. Nevertheless, he approached the stage with caution, pausing in the shadow to scan the environment before proceeding to the vehicle.

A careful search revealed nothing that could be considered of significance; but a few yards farther along the trail a big tree branch hung unnaturally low across the track, so that the men on the high seats of the coach would have had to bend low to avoid being scraped by the rough bark. Examination showed that a rope ran from the limb to the tree trunk and had been drawn taut, dragging the branch down over the trail.

"Simple and smart, horse," he told Shadow. "Just enough to throw the driver and the messengers off guard for a moment. Before they straightened up, they got it. Snake-blooded hellions! Murder means nothing to them. Looks like we should be in for an interesting time in this section."

Shadow snorted disapproval of the whole business, but his rider did not appear displeased with the prospect before him. In fact he wasn't, and welcomed the chance to match wits and guns with the ruthless outfit responsible for the murder of the two messengers and possibly the driver. He rode on, his face bleak, his eyes coldly gray.

While he was still many miles from Cholla, the dawn broke in a glory of scarlet and gold. He rode on for another hour, spotted a tall bristle of thicket with a trickle of water running past it, several hundred yards from the trail and turned aside. In the shelter of the growth he kindled a small fire of dry wood. From his saddle pouches he took a rasher of bacon, some eggs, carefully wrapped against breakage, and a hunk of bread. Soon coffee was bubbling in a little flat bucket, bacon sizzling in a small skillet. The eggs were fried to a consistency that would appear to cause certain indigestion to a rhinoceros. Slade ate his simple meal, while Shadow cropped grass that grew under the brush. Then, after washing the utensils, the Ranger curled up with his saddle for a pillow and was almost instantly asleep.

He was awakened shortly after noon by a drumming of hoofs on the distant trail. Peering from his concealment, he saw a compact body of men riding hard to the north, quite likely the sheriff and his posse on their way to investigate the robbery. Slade watched them out of sight, then, warming what was left of the coffee, he made his breakfast from the steaming bucket and the remainder of his bread. He rolled a cigarette, smoked it in leisurely fashion and then saddled up and proceeded on his way at an easy pace. He was in no particular hurry and estimated he should reach Cholla not long after dark.

Moonlight like silver rain streamed through a thin gauze of cloud as Slade neared the lights of Cholla. Under its soft touch, the gaunt outline of the spires and crags of the Cholla Hills were blurred and mellowed and the weirdly brandished arms of giant cacti cast grotesque shadows over the arid sands, for Cholla sat at the edge of what was practically a desert.

To a chance watcher it would have seemed that the tall Ranger drifted through the moonlight on invisible wings, rather than rode. For Shadow was so black that only the shimmer of the moonlight reflected by his satiny coat told that he was there at all.

Slade was in a jovial mood and as he rode he softly sang a love song of old Spain, in a voice like golden wine gushing into a crystal goblet.

In the Mexican quarter of the Border town, the *peons* lifted their heads, and tired eyes brightened as the rich voice came borne to them on the wings of the wind.

"El Halcon! The Hawk!" they murmured.

"*Ai*," said an old-timer. "El Halcon! He rides again! And he sings. *Ai*! When he sings some evil one will weep!"

Slade did not pause in the Mexican quarter, although hands were waved in greeting and soft-voiced invitations sounded as he passed the humble dwellings. He only waved a sinewy hand in reply, his even teeth flashing startlingly white in his bronzed face.

It was contagious, that white grin, and the *peons* smiled and laughed, and somehow the squalid quarter seemed brighter for his passing.

Only once did he pull the big horse to a halt—when a little girl with great liquid black eyes toddled out into the road. He leaned over, swept the crowing baby high into the air in the crook of one long arm and ruffled her black curls. Gently he set her down again in the moon-streaked dust, and she pattered back to her beaming mother, prattling delightedly and holding up a "souvenir" of her brief visit with El Halcon—a shiny .45 cartridge, with the powder removed.

"Reckon the first thing in order, horse," Slade said as he rode on, "is to find some place where you can bed down and put on the nosebag. I can stand a bite myself, and I figure you must be getting kind of lank, too, you dadblamed old grass burner!"

Shadow snorted general agreement and pricked his ears. Slade tickled his sensitive ribs with his spurs and Shadow squealed his anger and reached for a leg with gleaming teeth. Slade affectionately slapped his glossy neck and they ambled on in mutual good humor; the pair understood one another.

"Appears to be quite a pueblo," Slade added as lights began to appear with greater frequency and a babble of sound pierced through the monotonous drumming beat which continuously trembled the air. That pounding rumble, Slade knew, was the never-ceasing dance of the giant stamps pulverizing the gold ore taken from the mines in the Cholla Hills, at whose base the town was built.

Just as he knew that the lively thumping sounding from the garishly glittering street he was approaching was made by the muddy boots of the men who worked the mines.

"But those heels that are clicking on the floor like a lady cayuse's hoofs on a frozen trail haven't any mud on them," he told the black horse.

Shadow's answering snort seemed to indicate scant approval of the girls whose short skirts were swaying alongside the clumping boots; but his rider chuckled and his eyes grew merry with a light of anticipation.

"Oh, dance-floor girls aren't so bad, some of them," he disagreed. "Especially after you've looked at them a few times through the bottom of a glass. Funny how *señoritas* all seem to look the same through the bottom of a glass. Oh, well, if that's the way you feel about it, I won't argue with you anymore. Don't blow your nose off!"

Other clicking sounds became apparent as they drew abreast of the lighted windows. There was the musical clink of bottle necks against glass rims, the sprightly patter of dice across the green cloth, the soft slither of cards, the merry chatter of roulette wheels. Song, or what passed for it, bellowed forth; the soft thrum of guitars, the whine of fiddles and the pinging of banjos provided cheerful melody for the dancers, and the thumping of hard fists on the "mahogany" furnished even more cheerful music for the saloonkeepers. Evidently there was plenty of loose money in the town, Slade reflected, as he passed a solidly constructed building with "Bank" legending the windows. There was gold coming out of the hills, as the steady pound of the stamp mills attested. Which meant that other things would come out of the hills, things which interested the Ranger. Things which looked to be men but which could boast more than a fair allotment of snake blood, as the recent outrage on the trail just south of Harding could attest.

Glancing down a side street, he turned the black's head. A few moments later he pulled up in front of a small livery stable. Slade shouted and the sliding door creaked open on its rollers.

The owner of the stable wasn't small. He was tall, wide and thick, with twinkling little brown eyes set in rolls of fat. His face was rubicund, his mouth a pursed button, and there were chuckle-quirks at the corners and grin wrinkles around his eyes.

"Okay," he squeaked in a voice like a packrat with its tail caught in a crack.

Slade sent Shadow through the doorway and dismounted. "All right, Shadow," he said as the big horse laid his ears back. The fat man nodded approval. "Don't 'low anybody to touch him without an okay from you, eh?" he remarked. "I like that sort," he added as he deftly shucked off saddle and bridle and conducted Shadow into a stall.

"The sort it's worth getting hanged for to steal," the fat man piped, running an admiring glance over the horse's beautiful lines.

Slade grinned, after he had unscrambled the sentence.

"I gather you're not insinuating anything personal," he replied, "but I agree with the general sentiment."

"Name's Oakes," said the fat man in conversational tones, "mostly known as Sliver."

Slade supplied his own name and they shook hands gravely. Then Sliver Oakes busied himself caring for the horse. Slade watched him for a moment.

"Guess I don't need to give you any instructions," he commented. "You appear to know your business."

"I do," Oaks answered succinctly. "Twenty

years of following a cow's tail, before I got too fat, another five of running this shebang. Reckon you know somethin' about the cow business, too; nice rig you're using."

El Halcon nodded easily. "Yes, I've thrown a rope or two in my time," he admitted. He did not miss Oakes' glance at his hands and spread them wide, palms up.

"No, I haven't thrown one for quite a spell, though," he added quietly.

Oakes' fat face flushed. "Wasn't meaning anything personal," he squeaked. "You know an old-timer in the cow business sort of gets so he notices things—you weren't slow at catching on to how my glims were pointed yourself."

Slade nodded again. "Reckon you know something about itchy feet," he said. "When a fellow gets to trailing his rope from one place to another he doesn't do over much work for a spell, so long as his dinero holds out." His keen eyes had noted how Oakes' gazed fixed for an instant on his thumbs and forefingers, which had slight callouses on them. He could almost hear Sliver Oakes muttering to himself—"But you didn't get *those* callouses settin' on your hands. Maybe you haven't done much cow chambermaiding for a spell, but you've sure been practicing a fast draw."

However, Slade only said, "Any place around close where I could get a room?"

Oakes favored him with another shrewd glance,

hesitated, appeared to make up his mind to something.

"I have a room for rent above the stalls," he said at length. "Two up there; I use one."

"That will be fine," Slade replied. "I'll put my rig in it, if you don't mind."

"Okay," said Oakes. "And you don't hafta."

"Don't have to what?"

"Don't hafta pay in advance. Mostly I make young range riding hellions plank down the pesos first."

"Folks sort of on the dishonest side hereabouts?"

"Oh, I reckon they're about as fair to middlin' honest as in any section, but this is sort of an unhealthy locality, especially for young fellers with itchy trigger fingers who are looking for excitement. But if something breaks, I figure *you'll* look at the right end of your guns before you look into the wrong end of the other feller's. First door at the head of the stairs. I'll give you a key to the front door. Try and come in quiet, if you stay out too late and ain't too drunk."

Slade chuckled as he unscrambled that one, and ascended the stairs at the rear of the stable. The room at the head of the stairs was small but clean; the bunk looked comfortable. He deposited his rig and his rifle in a corner and returned to the stalls.

"Here's the key to the front door," said Oakes. "I don't often give one out, but I'll take a chance this time."

"Why?" Slade asked as he accepted the key.

"Because a feller that rides this sort of a horse can't be too bad," squeaked Oakes. "Suppose you're looking for a drink?"

"Something to eat would come closer to filling the bill right now," Slade replied.

Oakes jerked his head understandingly. "Nothing like eating," he said. "If you hanker for good chuck, mosey around the corner and down the main street to Carry Farr's Brandin' Pen. Drinks are okay, too. The girls are better than most and the games are as straight as Farr can keep them. Got a good Mexican orchestra there, too, for the dancing, and some fellers that can sing. Carry Farr's place is okay, 'cept a sorta salty crowd hangs out there."

"Carry Farr? A funny sounding name," Slade observed as he turned to the door.

"Uh-huh, 'Dot and Carry' is what the boys call him—you'll know why when you see him walk— but that's considerable of a mouthful, so folks mostly compromise on Carry."

Slade left the stable pondering the rather unusual character that was its owner. One, he felt, it would be wise to cultivate. He had a notion that if anything was going on, Sliver Oakes would know about it as quickly as the next. Those twinkling eyes in their rolls of fat didn't miss much, and there was a shrewd brain back of them. He wondered just where Oakes stood in relation to the various denizens of Cholla, and decided he would do well to try and find out. He suspected that Oakes' random talk had been for the purpose of feeling *him* out for some reason of his own. Which was interesting.

Slade had no difficulty locating the Branding Pen Saloon. He pushed through the swinging doors still curious about the proprietor's peculiar name.

The Branding Pen was a big place, fairly well-lighted and crowded. An orchestra of guitars and muted violins was making music for the dancers who were gathered on the open space to one side of the poker tables and the roulette wheels. There was a lunch counter, tables along one wall for the accommodation of more leisurely diners, and a bar which stretched the full length of the opposite wall. Several perspiring barkeeps were pouring drinks at top speed. Gold was clinking on the mahogany and more gold gleamed dully on the green cloth of the tables. The dance floor was busy and the girls, many of them Mexicans, were good-looking and young. Slade eyed them appreciatively.

And at the same time his gaze did not fail to note the swift appraising glances cast in his direction from various sources as he entered the saloon. Quite obviously, the habitués of the Branding Pen didn't miss any bets and were perhaps a bit leery of strangers.

A couple of Mexicans in black velvet adorned with much silver courteously made room for him and a fat jolly bartender sloshed whiskey into a ready glass. Slade downed his drink, called for another and as he toyed with it, casually scanned the reflections in the big back-bar mirror.

One thing instantly attracted his attention—the unusual quiet of the place. Men spoke in subdued voices that did not carry beyond their immediate neighborhood. The players at the tables placed their bets without unnecessary comment. The music of the really excellent orchestra was soft and seductive. Even the feet of the dancers seemed to touch the floor lightly. The Ranger also noticed that in many there was a litheness usually lacking in rock busters and pick-and-shovel men. Without a doubt, more than a few of the Branding Pen customers were riders. Range hands, or had once been. And Sliver Oakes was right; it was a salty gathering. But quite probably its members were good at attending to their own business, Slade reasoned, and they also would resent any meddlings in their affairs.

Slade finished his drink and sauntered to one of the tables ranged against the wall. As he sat down, a man come from behind the bar and started across the room toward the lunch counter; and El Halcon understood how the owner of the Branding Pen came by his nickname.

The man was powerfully built, with broad

29

shoulders, a deep chest and unusually long arms. But one leg was much shorter than its mate and the discrepancy gave him a most peculiar gait. He would take a step, seem to hesitate, take a half step, and then a full-length stride.

"Yes, 'dot and carry,'" Slade reflected. "That's just what it looks like he's doing."

He got a good look at Carry Farr's face as he passed under a light. It was a sinister appearing face, heavy of jaw, bulging of forehead, with a tight gash of a mouth, and pale eyes that peered coldly from under shaggy brows. And when Carry Farr's eyes flickered in his direction and looked him over with a suspicious, calculating gaze accompanied by a grim hardening of his thin lips, Slade's dark brows drew together slightly until the concentration furrow above the bridge of his high nose deepened, a sure sign that El Halcon was doing some thinking.

Slade finished his surprisingly good meal, rolled a cigarette and sauntered across the room to idle beside a roulette wheel near the Mexican dance orchestra. From time to time a young guitarist sang softly in a voice that was sweetly musical but lacked strength and made little impression. Absently he raised his gaze to the watcher, his dark eyes brightened with recognition and his teeth flashed in a smile. Impulsively he extended the guitar to Slade.

"*El Capitan* will sing?" he asked persuasively.

"Once before I heard him sing, and I have not forgotten. He will sing for us now? It would be the very great pleasure."

Half smiling, Slade shook his head; but others had noticed the young Mexican's gesture and had overheard his words.

"Come on, feller, give us a song!" shouted a gay young cowboy who held a tiny girl in his arms, her dark head coming hardly to his shoulder. She, too, smiled persuasively at the tall man who hesitated at the edge of the dance floor.

Other voices took it up. "You must be able to spout a good one, feller, if Miguel asks you to," declared a brawny miner. "Come on, don't be bashful."

Slade grinned, reached for the guitar and swept his slim fingers across the strings. He played a soft prelude, then threw back his black head and sang—sang that old, old song of the Southwest so dear to the inhabitants of *Mañana* Land, that song of longing and heartache and pathetic hope that Yradier wrote and named "The Dove."

Men hushed their talk at the bar and turned, glass in hand, to stare at the singer. The roulette wheels whirred to a halt, and nobody noticed where the bouncing balls had come to rest. A gambler laid down an ace-full, wrong side up, and left it that way. With one accord the dancers stilled their steps and stood motionless, the arms of the men still about the girls, and more than one pair of sinewy arms tightened their hold. Some of the girls tried to look careless. Others gazed from eyes that were dampened by a mist of dead dreams. Some, including the tiny dark-haired dancer, let the tears fall unashamed.

Dot-and-Carry Farr stood behind the bar, great red hands resting on its shining surface, his hard face as twisted as his grotesque body. The hands tightened into iron-hard fists, and in the cold eyes there was stark misery as he stared at the singer, gloriously straight and tall as a young pine of the forest.

With a last whisper of melody and a crash of chords, song and music ended, and for a tense moment the room was utterly silent. Then a thunder of applause burst forth, dying slowly, abruptly stilling as a harsh voice rasped balefully, "Mighty purty! I wouldn't be surprised, feller, if you could dance, too. Come on, give us a couple of steps. Come on! I ain't used to waiting on purty boys when I tell 'em to do something."

The audience, engrossed in the song, had not noticed the hulking giant who had lunged through the swinging doors and lurched to the far end of the dance floor to stand scowling blackly at the singer, his thick lips writhing back from big yellow teeth in a sneer, blunt fingers of one enormous hand caressing the black butt of one of the two heavy guns he wore sagging low, butts to the front, the mark of a cross-pull man.

But Walt Slade had noticed his entrance and had made a swift estimate of the new arrival, Drunk, or looks to be. Drunk and ugly, and plumb bad at any time.

Now, however, he smiled pleasantly at the speaker, although his eyes were no longer laughing but the slate gray of stormy water. He shook his black head.

"Nope, these boot heels are too high for dancing," he declined.

A dance girl giggled; somebody sniggered beside the bar. The newcomer's face darkened still more, his lip lifted in an animal-like snarl.

"Yeah? Well, I'll just shorten them a bit for you."

The big blue gun seemed to fairly leap from its holster, the black muzzle jutting toward Slade's feet.

From the guitar sounded a booming chord as Slade's fingers swept across the strings in a flashing blur of movement. In the crowded room a gun boomed with a sodden hollowness. Then, still smoking, it flashed back into its holster and the second chord of "Days of Forty-nine," absolutely in tempo, boomed forth.

THREE

The giant at the end of the dance floor was reeling back, gripping at his streaming right hand. His gun, the lock battered and smashed by the heavy slug from Slade's Colt, slammed against the bar and thudded to the floor, yards distant. Through the booming chords of the guitar Slade's voice sounded, clear as falling water, deadly as the hiss of a rapier blade, "Don't reach for the other one. I might miss next time, and I always miss *inside* a man's gunhand."

The big man did not reach for his second gun. He was too white and sick for that; a forty-five slug through the hand is no light matter. He reeled drunkenly for a moment, steadied himself and glared unbelievingly at the man who still stood impassively thrumming the guitar and smiling pleasantly. Once he opened his mouth, and twice, but no words came forth. A third attempt, and his harsh voice, thickened by pain and fury, gutturaled across the room: "Blast you, this ain't finished!"

He wheeled and lurched through the swinging doors, blood dripping to the floor in a steady stream. The night swallowed him and a babbling whirl of words filled the room.

"Blazes! What shooting! Crony had his hogleg out and lined!"

"And that feller never even stopped playing his guitar!"

And did you get that about missing *inside* the other feller's gunhand? I'd hate to have him 'miss' me that way. Who in the name of Pete is he, anyhow?"

"The only fellers I ever heard tell of who could shoot that way were John Ringo and Curly Bill Brocius," remarked an old-timer at the bar.

"Both dead years ago. Wyatt Earp killed Curly Bill at Iron Springs, over in Arizona. Ringo shot himself through the head."

"Uh-huh, that's how the story goes, but plenty of folks will tell you it ain't so, that those jiggers slid out of Arizona when it got too hot there and the pickings were getting slim. They'll tell you that neither of 'em is dead and are liable to show up anywhere."

"They'd both be a lot older now than that feller looks to be."

"Them owlhoot killers don't ever get to look old. The Devil keeps 'em looking young for his own purposes."

"You're loco!"

Nevertheless, speculative glances were cast at Slade, and eyes grew thoughtful.

"If those jiggers don't happen to be dead, I've a notion they wouldn't hanker to have folks blabbin' about them promiscuous, either one of 'em," somebody remarked. "Me, I wouldn't hanker to be doing something they wouldn't like."

There was silence.

Apparently oblivious of the babble, although his keen ears caught much of what was said, Slade handed the guitar to its owner.

"Who was that nice gent who just left?" he asked.

"That is the *Señor* Park Crony," the guitarist replied. "He is the head foreman of the *Señor* Howard Hunter's big Last Nugget mine. The *Señor* Hunter is *bueno*, but the *Señor* Crony! *Muy malo hombre!*"

Slade was willing to agree that Park Crony was really a "very bad man." As to whether Howard Hunter was good, his judgment would be held in abeyance until he learned more about him. With a smile and a nod, he returned to the table he had formerly occupied, which was not directly in line with any of the windows. He sat down, ordered a drink and pondered the seemingly senseless incident.

Not so senseless, perhaps, as it appeared to be. Could have been a well thought out plan to do him in. Fire a bullet close to his feet and when he resented the ill-advised display of humor, so called, and reached for his own gun, drill him dead center before he could line sights, and claim self-defense. If Crony had friends in the place who would back up his claim, he might well have

36

gotten away with it. Where he slipped, if a killing was really his object, was in not realizing that when a man drew a gun on El Halcon, retaliation would be instant and sure; explanations, if any were forthcoming, would have to wait until the matter at hand was attended to. In fact, the only reason that Park Crony was still alive was because Slade had not been quite sure that the affair was not merely the dangerous prank of a drunken individual with a perverted sense of humor.

Just the same, the business had a sinister look and smacked of the ingenious simplicity of the tree branch dragged low over the trail to distract the attention of the stage driver and its guards. Perhaps the outlaws had gotten a better look at him than he thought when he tangled with them on the Apache Trail and were out to even up the score. Could be! Slade shrugged his wide shoulders and sipped his drink.

Carry Farr crossed the room at his grotesque, sidling gait and paused beside the young guitarist of the orchestra. Slade could not hear the conversation that followed; it would have interested him.

"Miguel," said Farr, "just what do *you* know about that big jigger?"

"*Patron*," Miguel replied, "he is a strange man. Out of the nowhere he comes, into the nowhere he goes. He has killed men, yes, but only those who had already lived too long. Where there is trouble, sorrow, mistreatment, he appears, and when he departs he leaves peace and happiness behind. Many will tell you, and they are evil ones, that he is *El Diablo* himself, an outlaw who is too smart to get caught. Others, and they too are many, say different. They say—"

"I see," Carry Farr said thoughtfully. "*Gracias*, Miguel." He turned and sidled across to where Slade sat. The Hawk saw him coming but did not raise his head until Farr's harsh voice grated on his ears. Then he let his eyes rest on the saloon-keeper's sinister face. And as he did so, he noted something his rather casual former inspection had passed over, something that interested him.

"Feller," said Farr, "I'd like to have a little talk with you, in my back room, where we won't be interrupted. I think it will be to your interest to come along and gab with me a spell," he added meaningly.

Slade nodded without comment. Silently he followed Farr to the back room, the door to which opened near the end of the bar. Farr closed the door and locked it, and motioned to a chair beside a table on which rested a bottle and glasses.

"Who the devil *is* he?" a voice at the bar demanded querulously as the door closed. "And why's Dot and Carry nosing up to him that way? Gents, somehow I got a feeling that things are

38

going to get lively in the Branding Pen, livelier than ord'nary. Who is he?"

There was a general shaking of heads. Miguel, the guitarist, who might have enlightened them somewhat, smiled enigmatically, and held his peace. A lanky, hard-featured man who had been listening intently to the conversation but taking no part in it glanced at the closed door and sauntered out.

FOUR

Even as the door closed behind Slade, another man was riding into town. He was a blocky, sturdily-built old man with hard, intolerant eyes peering from under shaggy brows. He had a mouth and a jaw that promised a plentiful supply of that delightful quality called firmness in the fellow who's doing the talking, and mule-headed stubbornness in other folks. He sat his horse in an uncompromising fashion and gripped the reins as if he expected the cayuse to bolt at any moment and was prepared to bring him up short before he got away with any darn foolishness.

He was powdered from head to foot with dust and appeared to be in anything but a pleasant humor. Even the big nickel badge on the left breast of his sagging vest winked balefully in the moonlight.

The rider did not pause at the Branding Pen, although in passing he glowered at the saloon as if it were a personal affront. He rode on farther up the street and pulled his tired horse to a halt in front of a bigger, brighter, more elegantly-appointed establishment. With a grunt he swung to the ground and bellowed an order to a hanger-on nearby, who came forward obsequiously to lead the horse to a stable. With another grunt that apparently held some meaning for the grunter, the old man entered the saloon, blinking owlishly in the glare of light.

"Hi-yuh, Sheriff!" called a voice. "Come on over and set."

With a third grunt, which merged into a snort, the sheriff stumped solidly across the big and busy room and sat down at a table occupied by two men.

"Howdy, John. Howdy, Hunter," he rumbled, reaching for the glass a waiter instantly placed at his elbow.

"Any luck, Wes?" asked the man who had called the invitation.

Sheriff Wesley Cole snorted like a stallion with a burr under its tail. His face wrinkled with anger and disgust. He frowned at the speaker.

"Trying to be funny, John?" he demanded. "I didn't bring anybody back with me, did I?"

Old John Mosby, owner of the big Comstock mine and the Swinging J ranch, remarked, "I've known you to have plenty of luck in an outlaw hunting and *not* bring anybody back with you."

The sheriff grunted in a mollified tone. "Well, I didn't have any this time," he growled. "I didn't bring the hellions back, and I didn't leave any of them out on the desert or up in the hills, either. Didn't see hide or hair of 'em. I sent Deputy Short and some of the boys west and south by way of the waterholes over there, telling them to circle back east toward Harding on the chance the hellions headed for Mexico. I followed the Apache Trail back south myself. Maybe the other boys had some luck, but I'm not over hopeful."

"Short and his posse got in a couple of hours back," remarked the second man at the table.

Sheriff Cole grunted at the speaker, and drained his glass before commenting.

Howard Hunter was a handsome man with yellow hair inclined to curl and worn rather long, snapping eyes of clear blue, and regular features. He was lean and broad-shouldered, slim of hips and waist, in marked contrast to the blocky sheriff and the squat, ungainly owner of the Comstock mine.

Sheriff Cole sucked the drops from his mustache. "They *would!*" he snorted.

Old John Mosby's round face darkened with anger. He hit the table a resounding blow with a fist like an over-smoked ham.

"Something's got to be done!" he declared. "Do you realize this makes three gold shipments lost in the past four months? Nigh onto thirty thousand dollars this time, and two good men killed, and Hank Givens, the driver, hovering between life and death, judging from what Doc Cooper wired. I gather if Doc pulls him through, it'll be a miracle. I tell you something's got to be done about those infernal Cholla Raiders, as some darn fool named 'em."

Sheriff Cole suddenly looked very tired and old. "You're right, John, but what?" he asked heavily. "I'm doing all I can, but I don't seem to have any luck."

"I know you are, Wes," nodded Mosby. "It's a tough chore."

"I don't know how they worked it, but it was a smart and plumb daring holdup," said the sheriff. "Just a few miles this side of Harding. Another hour and that gold shipment would have been on the train and safe. Hank said, when he finally got his senses back, that there was a big tree branch hanging low over the trail. Him and the guards had to duck down to get under it and right then the hellions cut loose at them. Guards never had a chance."

"How come a branch was down that way?" wondered Mosby. "Don't recollect ever noticing one like that and I've rode that way lots of times."

Sheriff Cole rumbled angrily. "A plumb smart trick," he said. "The hellions tied a rope to it, pulled it down and fastened the rope around the trunk of the tree. Rope wouldn't be noticed in the dark, of course. I saw it when me and the boys rode by in daylight."

"Well, I'll be hanged!" sputtered Mosby. "You talked to Hank?"

"Uh-huh," the sheriff nodded. "He's mighty weak, but Doc let him talk a little. He said he got one through the shoulder that knocked him off the seat to the ground. He said that a big black whiskered feller who 'peared to be the leader of the bunch leaned over in his saddle and shoved a gun against his head and pulled the trigger. Funny what happened. Hank looked like he'd been drilled dead center, but I reckon the gun was held at an angle, so the bullet scooted along the bone just under the skin and came out over his ear. Shock knocked him out, of course, and the devil must have figured he was done for. Doc thinks he should pull through."

"The snake-blooded scoundrel!" swore Mosby. "By the way, how did Hank get to Doc's office if he was knocked out?"

"That's another funny one," said the sheriff. "Doc said a feller in cowhand clothes brought him in. Saved his life, according to Doc. Feller told him he had a run-in with a bunch on the trail, that they threw lead at him and he threw some back and downed one of them before they hightailed."

"That's good!" exclaimed Howard Hunter.

"Mebbe," the sheriff said dryly, "but I didn't find no body in the trail where the feller told Doc it would be. I found the bodies of the guards, and the stage, and the horses hanging around with the harness off, but that was all."

"And what does that mean?" Hunter wanted to know.

"It means," said the sheriff slowly, "that if the feller wasn't lying, the hellions came back later

44

and removed the body, so that nobody in Harding or here in Cholla would get a look at it."

"Meaning that they feared somebody would recognize the sidewinder," said Hunter.

"That's the way I see it, if that feller, whoever he was, wasn't lying," nodded the sheriff.

"What became of the feller?" asked Mosby.

Sheriff Cole shrugged. "Doc said he trailed his twine right after bringing Hank in," he replied.

"But why?" wondered Hunter.

"Guess, like everybody else, he didn't care to have it advertised that he tangled with the Cholla Raiders," answered the sheriff. "Those snakes have got everybody in the section buffaloed. Folks are scared to talk, if they know anything."

"Well, you can't much blame them," said Mosby. "A feller who came in and said he saw that bunch skalley-hootin' down Dry Water Canyon the night of the other stage robbery last month—you remember him, Hunter—and that he believed he'd know a couple of 'em if he saw them again was picked up in the alley back of the Branding Pen a little later with a knife between his shoulder blades. And one of my workers, a miner, was sounding off about the Cholla Raiders. Next day we found him at the bottom of a shaft where he had no business to be. Must have been grabbed and packed to the hole and dumped in."

Sheriff Cole scowled blackly. "The Branding Pen!" he exclaimed with a vicious snap. "Some

45

day I'll bust that rumhole open wide enough to drive a freight wagon through without scraping a hub. It's a owlhoot hangout or there never was one. And I got a good notion who's the he-wolf of the pack."

"Now, Wes, you have no right to say such a thing about Carry Farr," Howard Hunter chided gently. "There's no proof of any wrongdoing against Farr."

"And I figure the only reason there ain't is because he's too blasted smart to get caught—so far," retorted the sheriff. Hunter shook his head deprecatingly and said no more.

"This town needs more places like your Cattlemen's Club here, Howard," the sheriff rambled on. "A decent saloon and eating place where folks can enjoy themselves and not be scared of stopping lead is a credit to the community."

He glanced around the well-filled, comparatively quiet room as he spoke, his eyes appreciating the orderly arrangements, the shining glassware, the well-stocked back-bar.

"But a joint like the Branding Pen!" he concluded. "Well, I'm going to wash up before I eat. See you in a few shakes. He levered his bulky body from the chair and stalked across the room. Old John Mosby watched him go.

"Yes, something's got to be done," he repeated when the sheriff was out of earshot. "It isn't only the stage robberies and the one at the bank. The widelooping of highgrade ore from my mine is even worse, from my way of looking at it. Production has fallen off a full thirty per cent of paying ore in the past six months. I *know* the stuff is coming out of the veins, but it isn't reaching the mill. I've tried every way I know to run the hellions down, but haven't had any luck. Put some fellers I *knew* I could trust working alongside the muckers and rock men. Right away three of them get smashed beneath a rock fall that had no business falling. Another killed by a dynamite blast that went off prematurely for no reason anybody could figure. No, it isn't so much the shipments we've been losing which, after all, were partly insured, that bothers me, it's the highgrade I know I'm losing."

For a moment the two men sat silent. Mosby was right about the constant drain on his resources. A quartz mine has a tremendous overhead and the percentage of profit to the owner is seldom unusually large. Very often the difference between gain and loss depends on the pockets of highgrade ore that spot the veins, ore often amazingly rich in metal. The average output of the veins may little more than pay expenses, sometimes not even that. If a large portion of his highgrade is steadily purloined, he may well face financial ruin. Small wonder Mosby was worried.

Howard Hunter's handsome face also wore a

worried look. "Maybe the shipments don't matter so much to you, but they matter plenty to me," he said. "My Last Nugget isn't any Comstock, and what I lost out of those shipments hurts."

Mosby nodded and glanced about the busy saloon. "You got a paying proposition here," he commented with apparent irrelevance.

"Lucky for me I have," growled Hunter. "If it wasn't for the Cattlemen's Club, the Last Nugget would just about be closing down after this last raid."

"And I guess I'm lucky to have my spread, the Swinging J, to fall back on if things get too bad," chuckled Mosby.

Hunter nodded. "But you're right, something has to be done," he said.

Mosby glanced in the direction of the wash-room, saw nothing of the sheriff and lowered his voice.

"I'm doing something," he announced sententiously. "Wes is a nice feller and salty, but he's getting old and maybe sort of losing his grip. And after all, he was just a cowman who got elected to office. Never had any peace officer training such as is needed to buck such an outfit as we are up against. I wouldn't want him to know what I'm telling you, because I'd hate to hurt his feelings. I sent a letter to Captain Jim McNelty of the Rangers week before last asking him to send some men over here."

Hunter leaned forward eagerly, his eyes snapping. "That was smart," he said. "What did McNelty have to say?"

Old John snorted his anger and disgust. "Wrote me he couldn't very well spare a bunch of men right now, what with the trouble along the Border over to the west, and such. Said he'd detail a man or two to this section sometime later, if possible. Said the matter concerned was something the local authorities should be able to handle, so far as he could make out, but that he'd lend a hand when he was able. Heck of a note! But maybe this last robbing and killing may make him stir his stumps a little. Forget it, now; here comes Wesley."

"Right," said Hunter. "Well, guess I'd better circulate around among the boys a bit; can't afford to neglect the personal touch, you know."

He left the table and sauntered about the room, saying a word here and there, pausing with a ready smile for newcomers and a moment of conversation. Some little time elapsed before he returned to the table, where Sheriff Cole was putting away a bountiful meal.

FIVE

Just as the sheriff was knifing a final slab of pie under his mustache, a huge man entered the saloon and slouched across the room to the table. His face was twisted with pain and his right hand, elaborately bandaged, was suspended in a sling.

Howard Hunter stared at him in amazement. "What the devil happened to you, Crony?" he demanded.

The big man slumped into a chair and growled an order to a waiter.

"Feller shot me," he rumbled.

Now both the sheriff and Hunter stared; John Mosby whistled.

"You mean to tell us," sputtered the peace officer, "that somebody busted *your* gunhand with a slug?"

Park Crony mutter-gurgled through his drink what was evidently intended for assent.

"Slip up behind you or something?" Hunter asked quietly.

Crony set down his glass and glared. "I got my faults, Boss," he replied, "plenty of 'em, that I'm not denying, but lying and making excuses aren't some of 'em. I'm not going to tell any fancy, highfalutin yarn about how this jigger got me at a disadvantage or something like that. He just naturally pulled so fast he blew my hogleg outa my hand before I could crook finger."

The sheriff made a noise like a too-cropful rooster. Hunter leaned forward, his blue eyes gleaming. "Suppose you start at the beginning," he suggested.

Crony grunted and ordered another drink. "I was drunk," he prefaced.

"That isn't news," Hunter interrupted sarcastically.

"I was drunk on my own time," Crony blazed. "I don't drink during working hours and you know it, and I handle my job as it should be handled." He glared hot resentment at his employer, but his angry gaze wavered and shifted before Hunter's cold blue glitter.

"Yes, I was drunk," he repeated, "but not so drunk I couldn't handle myself." His gaze met Hunter's squarely. "You know when I get drunk I sometimes get sort of playful."

The sheriff's snort interrupted him, and after the peace officer's fragmentary bumble about "barb-wired bulls with burrs under their tails," Crony went on talking.

"I was feeling playful and sort of outa sorts when I ambled into that rumhole of Carry Farr's. There was a feller in there singing. A sort of purty-boy feller with black hair and the kind of eyelashes that are an inch long and look like they'd been dusted with soot. He was playing a

51

guitar and singing a Mexican song, singing it mighty well, too. I didn't like him. Reckon he was too darned good looking or something with those snapping eyes and that hawk nose." Crony's own ugly face twisted and glowered. "No, I didn't like him. I took a notion it would be sort of nice to have him give the bunch a bullet dance. Well, it didn't work. I had my iron in my hand and was just throwing down on one of his fancy high heels when he let me have it. I got just a flicker of that gun coming out and lining, but it wasn't any use. Before I could pull trigger my gun was half-way across the room and my hand busted. And that hellion never even stopped playing his infernal guitar!"

There was a moment of astounded silence.

"That blankety-blank Branding Pen!" raved the sheriff. "Didn't I tell you it's the hangout for all the owlhoots in this end of Texas!"

Howard Hunter leaned forward, his eyes sparkling with interest. "The man who shot you," he prompted, "was he quite tall, wide in the shoulder, with gray eyes?"

"Don't know what color his blasted eyes were, but when they're looking through powder smoke they're bad, plumb bad. Yes, he was a big hellion, plenty tall. Not big like me, but plenty big."

"And you say he was playing a guitar and singing?"

"That's right."

"Wish I knew what color horse he rides," muttered Hunter.

"He didn't bring it into the saloon with him, so far as I know," Crony remarked with ponderous sarcasm.

Hunter didn't appear to notice. He leaned back in his chair, his eyes thoughtful.

"I've a notion I've heard of that man," he said slowly. "If he's the man I'm thinking about, he's been riding through southwest Texas for quite a spell. Always seems to be around when something particularly off-color and salty is pulled, but there's never been anything tied on him, so far as I ever heard. The Mexicans call him *El Halcon*."

"That means The Hawk in Spanish," Mosby interpolated. Hunter nodded.

"Has an extremely fine singing voice, and an extremely fast gunhand, from what I've heard," Hunter commented reflectively.

"If that sidewinder who shot me is the one you're thinking about, I can vouch for the fast gunhand part," growled Crony. "Have to admit his singing sounded sort of purty, too."

"I've a very strong notion he's El Halcon, all right," said Hunter.

"Guess you'd better look over your reward notices, Wes," put in Mosby.

Sheriff Cole tugged his mustache. "I rec'lect something about a feller called El Halcon, too," he said. "Gather he's an owlhoot, all right, but that nobody has ever been able to get anything on him. If I remember right, he's got quite a few killings to his credit, but somehow the jiggers he killed always seemed to have it coming. What you getting at, Howard?" he asked of Hunter, who still looked reflective.

"Nothing definite," the Last Nugget owner replied. "Only it seems that the few folks who happened to get a look at the infernal Cholla Raiders and stayed alive saw that the man who appears to be the leader of the outfit is big and tall with short black whiskers."

"Feller who shot me didn't have no whiskers," grunted Crony.

"Whiskers can be shaved," Hunter pointed out. "And some men can grow a pretty fair crop in a week. Also, it is said that the hellion rides a fine black horse. Which is also said of El Halcon."

"All horses look black at night, the only time the Cholla Raiders have ever been spotted," said the sheriff. "That is all except white or gray broncs, and I never heard of that sort of an outfit going in for ghost-colored horses.

"Just the same," he added with a speculative gleam in his eyes, "it's something worth thinking on. And I think I'll have a talk with that gent who outdrew Crony."

SIX

In the back room of the Branding Pen, Carry Farr gestured to the bottle.

"Help yourself," he said. "My private stock. Got more rattlesnake juice and cactus spines in it than what I sell over the bar."

"Sounds fine," chuckled Slade, "but what I'd really like, if it isn't too much trouble, is a good hot cup of coffee."

"I like coffee, too," said Farr. "Wait a minute and I'll get a pot we'll share. And some sandwiches, too. Can always talk better when I've got something to eat handy."

Slade nodded, his eyes fixed on Farr's sinister face, seeming to see something there that interested him more than a little. Farr unlocked the door and passed out, closing it behind him. Shortly he reappeared with a waiter bearing a coffee pot with steam curling from the spout, cream, sugar, and a plate heaped with sandwiches of various sorts. He locked the door again after the waiter had departed.

"Light in," he invited. "We'll have our snack and then I have a few things to say to you, if you don't mind. As I said before, I think it will be to your interest to listen."

Slade did not comment beyond a nod. He and

Farr tackled the coffee and sandwiches, eating and drinking slowly, with no conversation other than a remark now and then on the food.

As he ate, Slade studied the room. It had one barred and shuttered window, and a second door, a key in the lock, that apparently led to the outside. The door was obliquely across from where he sat, almost opposite Farr. In one corner was a big iron safe, the door swung open.

Carry Farr intercepted his gaze. "Plenty of dinero in that old box, a whole week's take," he observed casually. He limped over to the safe, swung open the light inner door to reveal stacks of bills and rolls of gold coin.

"Would be wiser to keep the outer door shut and locked," Slade remarked as Farr closed the inner door and returned to his chair.

"Oh, the combination's hard to work, and the room doors are always locked," Farr replied carelessly. "Only my two bartenders, men I trust absolutely, have keys. Everything is under control."

Slade nodded. His interested gaze was again fixed on Carry Farr's face.

A half hour and more had passed when Farr leaned back in his chair, wiped his mouth with the back of his hand and shot Slade a quizzical glance.

"Guess you're wondering why I asked you to come back here and gab?" he remarked inter-rogatively.

"Well, I am a bit curious," Slade smiled in reply.

"Here it is," Farr said tersely. "Out in the other room I saw you out-draw Park Crony, who's said to have the fastest gunhand hereabouts, with possibly one exception."

"The exception?"

"Howard Hunter, his boss. Hunter is a gentleman; Crony isn't. Hunter owns the Last Nugget mine and the Cattleman's Club saloon. Crony is his mine foreman and general handy man. He's capable but mean. Hunter is capable, too, but not mean, so far as anybody has been able to notice, although he can be plenty salty if necessary. But here's the point. Watching you, I decided you're just the man I need to give me a hand here to keep order and the games straight. I'm offering you a job that'll pay better than following a cow's tail and give you more time to yourself, if—" Farr hesitated—"if you like to ride around and look things over. I'll only need you from midnight on to about five in the morning. I've got a good man as shotgun guard in the early hours, but he doesn't notice things like I've a notion you do. Around midnight the drinking slows and the big play at the tables begins, and goes on till daylight. I try to run straight games and I want them kept straight. It pays to do so. Take your regular house cut and you come out ahead in the end more than if you trim the suckers with crooked wheels and dealing. Trim 'em and they don't come back. Treat 'em square and they do. But it's not always easy to keep the dealers from pulling something now and then."

Farr paused to stuff tobacco in his pipe and light it. "I'm not concealing the fact that the job is sometimes a mite dangerous," he resumed. "I lost a lookout man two weeks back. He got one between the eyes and a jigger nobody had ever seen before, or would admit having seen, got a charge of buckshot that blew half his head off, but getting his scattergun in action before he died didn't help the guard. I lost another the same way a couple of months ago, and one a year back. But I figure you can take care of yourself. What do you say?"

Slade sat silent, turning the proposition over in his mind. It had attractive features. It would give him more time of his own than a job of riding possibly could, and he had a presentiment that the Branding Pen was very likely a focal point of the section's activities. Of course there was the chance that the offer might be a trap, cleverly baited; but he was confident that if that were the case, he could take care of anyone who sought to spring it. Once again his gaze rested on Carry Farr's sinister face.

"Looks like you've hired yourself a hand," he said.

Farr opened his lips to speak, but whatever he

had to say was drowned by another voice, a voice even more strident than his own, which grated unpleasantly on the ear—

"Okay, gents, stay put with your hands on the table like you are."

Farr started half out of his chair, and sank back, his hands rigid on the table top, quivering in every muscle. Slade made no move, other than a sideways flicker of his long gray eyes.

The door on the far side of the room, which had been closed, stood ajar, and through the crack protruded the yawning twin muzzles of a sawed-off shotgun.

For crawling seconds the drama held, suspended. The tense, deathly still moment when the fuse-fire licks the dynamite cap. The noises in the saloon beyond the closed door sounded suddenly loud and raucous, and very far away. Then the voice spoke again from out the dark.

"We're not interested in you, Farr—yet. You just set tight and don't make any funny moves. But that big feller is going with us. Steady, now, this scattergun ain't loaded with gooseberries!"

Soundlessly, the door swung farther open on oiled hinges. Two men, masked, hatbrims drawn low, sidled into the room, letting the door swing shut behind them. The leader held the shot-gun clamped against his hip. His companion had empty hands, but the black handles of heavy sixes flared out from his bulky hips.

The first man gestured to Slade with the cocked shotgun.

"Push your chair back slow," he ordered, "slow and easy, and stand up with your hands on the table. Then get 'em up slow, and high, and turn around and face the wall."

Slade obeyed, without argument. He got to his feet with apparent awkwardness because of the necessity of keeping both hands on the table, sidled away from the chair and half turned toward the wall, hands raising above his head. The man with the shotgun gestured to his companion.

"Get his hardware," he directed.

The other started forward, and for a fraction of a second he was almost between the table and the ready shotgun; and in that fraction of second Walt Slade acted. He whirled, one foot shot out and hooked under the chair rung. With all the strength of his muscular leg he slung the chair off the floor. It hurtled through the air toward the masked pair, spinning crazily. With a crashing boom, both barrels of the shotgun let go. The double charge of buckshot slammed into the heavy oaken seat of the chair, checking its flight as if it had been caught by a giant hand.

Slade went sideways through the smoke whorls, both guns blazing. Carry Farr joined in with a big Colt. The room seemed to explode with a roar of six-shooters. The shotgun clattered to the floor, its wielder slumped beside it with a choking grunt.

The second man had his guns out but the slugs from them splintered harmlessly into the floor as Slade laced two bullets through his heart and he pitched down beside his companion.

Before the echoes had stopped slamming between the walls, the hubbub in the outer room stilled as if blanketed by a snow slide. For a numbed instant the silence was absolute.

Carry Farr floundered across the room, amazingly swift for a crippled man. He scooped up the shotgun, jerked open the table drawer, slammed the weapon in and closed the drawer.

"No sense in letting everybody know the Cholla Raiders are after you," he snapped at Slade. "A sawed-off is their trade mark."

Now the outer room was a wild uproar of shouting and cursing. Boots pounded the floor, fists hammered the door with sledgehammer blows. Carry Farr limped to it, unlocked it and flung it open. Men peered, hesitated, boiled into the back room, exclaiming, questioning. Farr raised his hand to still the pandemonium. His harsh voice rang out.

"Just a try at a holdup," he said. "Didn't work. Slade here got the drop on the hellions before they could pull trigger."

He crab-gaited to the two dead outlaws and jerked the masks from their faces, revealing hard-bitten countenances distorted by the agony of death sudden and sharp.

"Anybody know them?" he asked.

Men leaned to peer close. One let out an exclamation. "Blazes!" he shouted. "This lanky one was drinking alongside me not an hour ago. I noticed him because of that wart on the end of his nose."

Another chorus of exclamations went up. Under cover of the excitement, Slade deftly righted the chair and shoved its buckshot-spattered seat out of sight under the table. Carry Farr let out a bellow and his two bartenders came hurrying to him.

"Which one of you left that back door unlocked?" he asked with deadly quiet. The barkeeps stared.

"Boss, it was locked when I came to work, I'll swear to it," one replied.

"And I ain't been in the back room all evening," protested the other. Farr surveyed them grimly.

"Well, it wasn't locked," he announced flatly. "I'll get to the bottom of this, and when I do, somebody will catch it."

Walt Slade was gazing at the door. He alone noticed that the key was in a locked position. He sauntered to the door, opened it and peered out, apparently searching the alley behind the saloon; his body hid the lock from those in the room.

A single glance showed him that the socket that should have received the bolt was empty. *The bolt had been removed from the lock.* He closed the door and came back to where the dead men lay, the exclaiming crowd still clustered about them.

"Here comes the sheriff!" whooped a young cowboy, delirious with excitement.

Sheriff Cole strode into the room, his eyes snapping. "What's been going on here?" he demanded harshly. Carry Farr looked him up and down with his cold eyes.

"Always the cow's tail, Wes," he replied. "Always behind. Never around when you're needed."

The sheriffs white mustache bristled in his scarlet face; he glared at Farr.

"Some day—" he began.

"Oh, yes, I know," Farr interrupted. "Some day you're going to close me up—some day! Sorry we didn't have time to send for you and had to take the law in our own hands, but those two gents there 'peared to be in a hurry and we were afraid they wouldn't wait."

That started the angry sheriff on another tack. He whirled to face Slade.

"And you!" he bawled. "You got a reputation for taking the law in your own hands. Why the devil did you have to show up here? Oh, I know, nobody has ever been able to get anything on you, but trouble just follows you around. Ain't I got enough without El Halcon squattin' here?"

A sudden hush fell over the crowd, broken by an old-timer's exclamation:

"El Halcon! That poor Park Crony!"

"You mean that lucky Park Crony," remarked another. "Still alive, ain't he?"

"I've always heard El Halcon never kills a man unless he has to."

"He's sure had to a lot, then."

"Uh-huh, and right there's a couple of samples of his killings. Only hope he gets a chance to do in a few more of the same sort."

"You can say that a couple of times, hombre."

Slade's lips twitched slightly; but the random remarks only added fresh fuel to the sheriff's fiery mood.

"I don't want you here!" he thundered. "You get out of town or I'll throw you in the calaboose."

"On what charge?" Slade asked mildly.

"I'll find one," declared the sheriff. "Being a general darn nuisance would do as well as any, I reckon."

Before Slade could reply, another voice spoke, a quiet, modulated voice with a singular carrying quality.

"Wes," it said, "you're talking out of turn and you know it. Bluster doesn't get anybody anywhere, especially in situations like this."

Slade had watched the tall, yellow-haired man enter the room and had been struck by the rhythmical perfection of his movement. He strode lithely but unhurriedly, and men made way for him. The foremost impression he gave was one of steely strength and self-confidence that verged on arrogance but lacking the irritating quality usually attributed to arrogance. It was just that the man was absolutely sure of himself, confident that his sizing up of a situation was correct in all angles. The sheriff cooled visibly.

"Guess you're right, Hunter," he grumbled, "but this feller *has* got a reputation for kicking up trouble wherever he shows."

Howard Hunter's well-formed lips shadowed a smile. "I know how you feel," he said gently, "in a mood to hit any head that shows; but flying off the handle won't help. I think it would be better to learn just what happened here before jumping at conclusions. I've a suspicion that Farr and this gent were absolutely in the right, and I think your better judgment will cause you to agree with me. You've had a harassing day and your nerves are on edge, which generally isn't the case."

"Well, I guess you're right again," the sheriff said in mollified tones. "Farr, just what did happen?"

Carry Farr told him, tersely, stressing the part Slade played in the affair. When he had finished, Sheriff Cole gazed at the tall Ranger with something approaching respect.

"Guess you were in the right this time," he said grudgingly. "But for Pete's sake lighten the latigo on your gunplay. Well, some of you fellers can pack the carcasses over to my office. I'll wire Doc Cooper, the coroner, to come down and hold an inquest, though there ain't no sense in it."

The bodies were carried out. Carry Farr locked the door to the saloon. As an afterthought he took a chair and jammed it under the knob of the door that led to the alley, the door which appeared to be locked but wasn't. Slade watched the operation, a slight pucker between his black brows.

"The way things are happening, I'm taking no chances," said Farr. "Nobody can get that one open again without making a racket. Sit down, I'll have some more coffee and sandwiches sent in. All this hullabaloo got me hungry again."

A little later, over the rim of his coffee cup, he regarded Slade silently for a long moment.

"Looks like, somehow, you've got yourself right up to the neck in the soup," he finally remarked. "Any notion why the Cholla Raiders are after you?"

"Don't like my face, perhaps," Slade evaded.

"Maybe," nodded Farr, "but I think I can make a better guess. Are you really El Halcon?"

"Been called that," Slade admitted carelessly.

"And with a reputation for horning in on things," Farr said slowly. "Yes, I think that's it. The hellions are scared you're here to take over the good pickings they've been enjoying."

"Could be," Slade smiled. "Still in the notion of taking me on as a floor man? Might bring trouble to you, if your guess happens to be correct."

Farr's face went grim. "I'll not worry about the

66

trouble," he answered. "I'm sort of used to trouble, have been all my life, and I ain't in the habit of sidestepping any that comes my way. The offer stands."

For the fourth time Slade studied Carry Farr's grotesque countenance. Suddenly he smiled, the flashing white smile of El Halcon that men as well as women found irresistible. Its warmth seemed to reflect in Farr's face, for the harsh lines softened a bit and the expression of his eyes changed.

"Sidestepping trouble often just means barging head-on into other trouble," Slade said. "And perhaps you're wrong about the Cholla Raiders being responsible for what happened tonight."

"Perhaps I am," replied Farr, his voice carrying no conviction, "but as I said before, a sawed-off shotgun is their trade mark. They've used one in every robbery and murder they've committed. A scattergun usually doesn't leave any witnesses."

Thinking of the buckshot-riddled bodies of the two stage guards, Slade was silent.

"Well, imagine you're tired and ready to hit the hay," observed Farr. "See you tomorrow evening. Sleep tight. Guess the Raiders are through riding for tonight."

A hush fell as Slade crossed the saloon with his long, swinging stride and all eyes followed him, those of the dance-floor girls with undisguised admiration.

"El Halcon!" murmured Miguel, the guitarist.

"Now let those whose hearts are not clean beware!"

It was in the dead dark hour just before the dawn that Walt Slade made his way back to his room in the little livery stable on the outskirts of the town. He was just turning toward the door when, borne on a vagrant breath of wind, there came to his ears a soft drumming. He located it as coming from the trail that ran from north to south to writhe through gloomy, mysterious Dry Water Canyon and wind on into the bleak fastnesses of the Cholla Hills.

Louder grew the sound, beating swiftly from the north. Slade focused his eyes on a gray fragment of trail that could be seen from where he stood. It shimmered faintly in the starlight, empty, lonely.

Then abruptly it was no longer empty. Huge, dark shapes, distorted and magnified in the illusive light, were drifting across the patch of gray—like the ghosts of long-dead dawns. As fantastically as they had appeared, they vanished, and only that hollow drumming was left to speak of their passing, a drumming which swiftly faded to a whisper of sound that died in the shadows to the southwest, shadows that seemed the blacker for the tremulous silver-gray which was welling upward in the eastern sky.

For long moments Slade gazed in the direction of the unheard sound. He spoke aloud as he turned to the stable door—

"Looks like the Cholla Raiders are *not* through riding for tonight."

SEVEN

"I tell you, you gotta pay in advance, after all!" squealed Sliver Oakes. "Any young hellion who takes such a job as shotgun guard in a snake hole like Carry Farr's Branding Pen ain't to be relied on to be here to pay his feed and room bill when it comes due. Collecting from estates is too darn much trouble."

Walt Slade, standing tall and lithe in the blaze of the noonday sun, chuckled as his merry eyes ran over the excited fat man.

"What's wrong with the Branding Pen?" he wanted to know.

"Oh, nothing, nothing at all!" Sliver replied with withering sarcasm. "The Sunday School and prayer meetings clutter it up awful, but otherwise it's fine. Nice place! Why, fellers have been known to have stayed alive in there for most of two hours! Such a nice, gentle outfit of horse thieves and wideloopers and owlhoots bed down there in perfect peace and get along with the sidewinders, Gila monsters and vinegaroons and tarantulas that have been chased out of the desert and clean from Arizona because they were too blasted ornery to be allowed to associate with the other varmints. Nice place! Shootings most every night. Understand you blowed a gun out of Park

69

Crony's hand there last night and downed a couple more horned toads. Fine beginning! You'll fit right in the joint, for so long as you'll last, which won't be long."

Slade shook with laughter. "You sure make out a fine case for the Branding Pen," he observed.

Sliver Oakes was abruptly grave. His voice modulated, deepened.

"That's just my way of talking," he said quietly. "But don't discount the Branding Pen and the people who hang out there. As perhaps you've heard, a lookout guard was killed in there a couple of weeks back. Incidentally, that makes the *third* lookout killed there in the past year. If you had to take a job working in a saloon, why didn't you make a try for Howard Hunter's Cattlemen's Club? That's a really nice place and sort of on the swell side. The barkeeps actually wear collars and shave twice a week. Howard Hunter's a gentleman, though he can be plenty salty if necessary. A lot different from Carry Farr."

"And besides owning the Branding Pen, what's the matter with Farr?" Slade asked casually.

Sliver Oakes hesitated. "Can't say as there's anything definite," he admitted. "Mexicans like him, and so do fellers who aren't getting along too well or who have had trouble. Old Doc Cooper, up at Harding—Doc spends a lot of time here, got a little office he uses for his coroner work and to patch up gents here now and then—Doc swears

70

Farr's worth a dozen Howard Hunters and even a couple of John Mosbys, despite the fact that Doc and Mosby, who owns the big Comstock mine, are purty good friends. But then Doc is sort of queer—hipped on book learnin', I reckon, and maybe touched in the head a little in consequence. The fact is, too many salty hellions from both sides the Border hang out in Carry's place and are on good terms with him. I'm not one to truck talk I'm not sure about, and what I'm telling you now is no personal opinion of mine." He glanced around and lowered his voice.

"There are folks who believe, and I'm afraid Sheriff Cole is one of them, that Carry Farr might be the big boss of the Cholla Raiders."

Slade kept his face expressionless. "The Cholla Raiders?" he repeated, interrogatively.

Again Oakes glanced about nervously, although there was nobody in sight, certainly not within hearing distance, and Slade noted curiously that his fat face was beaded with sweat. Sliver lowered his voice still more.

"Yes, the Cholla Raiders," he said, "a bunch that hangs out in the hills and swoops down when nobody is expecting them. There hasn't been a salty owlhoot job pulled in this section in the past six months but what the Cholla Raiders have been in it, or so everybody believes. Nobody knows who they are and folks who have been over curious about 'em haven't enjoyed particular good health. There was old man Chismy, who lost a big herd and got a posse of his riders together and set out after the Raiders. Was pressing 'em sort of hard, I gather, when all of a sudden the trail in the snow just stopped all of a sudden—it was early Spring and there'd been a light fall during the night that made tracking easy, which was why Chismy and his bunch were overhauling them. Yes, the trail all of a sudden wasn't there. Of course, it was an old trick—the owlhoots just doubled back careful to a thicket, brushed out their tracks that led into the thicket and laid low, but they did it so almighty slick that Chismy and his riders were thrown off guard for a minute, which was long enough. There him and his near a dozen other Solomons were, bunched up and showing hard and clear against a white cliff."

Sliver paused to roll a cigarette. Slade waited, expectant.

"Two of the Chismy boys lived long enough to tell what happened," Sliver concluded succinctly.

Slade nodded. "A salty outfit all right," he admitted, a cold and retrospective gleam in his gray eyes.

"That goes double," said Oakes. "Sheriff's been chasing himself around the county like a chicken with its head cut off, but he's got nothing to show for it but corns under the seat of his pants. Guess he'll take to riding herd on Carry Farr and the Branding Pen for a spell again, and meanwhile the

Cholla Raiders'll pull another job. Old Man Mosby, who owns the Comstock mine, swears that somehow they're responsible for the high-grade ore-stealing from his mine that's heading him to bankruptcy, though how he figures it I don't know."

"An outfit working over a section gets the blame for everything that happens, often to the advantage of the real culprits," Slade observed. "But speaking of Carry Farr, he's a lame man. Doesn't look like a man with one leg quite a bit shorter than the other could get by with such an outfit and not be noticed."

"That brings out a funny thing about the feller who bosses the outfit," said Sliver. "Nobody has ever seen him out of the saddle. His men do all the work that's necessary and he sits up in the hull and watches. Lends a hand when needed, but never comes down. Why, I heard that during the holdup of the stage down toward Harding night before last, he plugged the driver while old Hank was lying on the ground. Leaned over and leaned way down to shove the gun against his head. Didn't unfork as you'd expected a feller would for a job he wanted to make sure of. Feller is always husky looking, like Carry looks when he's on a horse, has black hair like Carry's got, and wears black whiskers like what maybe Carry could grow."

"Takes time to grow whiskers; he could hardly

do it running the Branding Pen without creating comment," Slade observed.

"Uh-huh, that's right," agreed Sliver. "But Carry is a feller who has a habit of riding off alone every now and then without telling anybody where he's going. Sometimes gone for as much as a couple of weeks. Cook, his head bartender, runs the place when he's gone and does a good job of it. Carry got back from one of those trips just yesterday afternoon; been gone all week. Just rode in without saying where he'd been or anything."

Slade nodded. The bit of information cleared up something that had been puzzling him—why should Farr have kept a whole week's take in his safe in the back room. Apparently the head bartender in charge had waited for Farr to make a deposit at the local bank.

Not yet resolved in his mind, however, was why Farr should have shown him, a stranger, the money. Perhaps to test him, although that appeared a bit far-fetched. He did recall that the saloonkeeper's shrewd eyes had never left his face while discussing the money.

Another intriguing angle was the boltless lock on the back door. Removing the bolt had undoubtedly been an "inside job" performed by somebody who had access to the back room. It could never have been removed from the outside. Slade was waiting with interest for somebody to mention that missing bolt.

And the matter of the sawed-off shotgun, the "badge" of the Cholla Raiders, which Farr had so quickly stowed out of sight. His explanation that it would be better to conceal the fact that Slade was a target of the Cholla Raiders had sounded a bit lame; but then, the obvious often sounds lame, because it is the obvious. All in all, Slade had not made up his mind concerning Carry Farr, although in the back of it an opinion was crystallizing.

"Heck, I'm talking like I was makin' out a case against Carry, which I'm sure not aiming to," concluded Sliver. "Fact is, I sort of like the hoppety-skip hellion, so maybe you'll make out all right with him. What you aim to do now?"

"First some breakfast, then I think I'll take a little ride," Slade replied; he was gazing toward the shadowy mouth of Dry Water Canyon, which in the waning starlight of the dawn had swallowed the mysterious band of night riders.

"A good notion," nodded Sliver, and profanely refused the "payment in advance" Slade proffered with vast solemnity.

Slade ate his breakfast at the Branding Pen. The food was excellent, the service good. Carry Farr was not yet in evidence, but he had evidently briefed the other employees as to Slade's status, for when he tried to pay for his meal he was told that the help always ate on the house.

"Mr. Farr's a good man to work for," said the waiter who served him. "Pays well and all he asks is that you be square with him and he'll be square with you. When you're right, he'll back you to the handle against anybody."

Slade was smoking a leisurely cigarette over a final cup of coffee when Carry Farr arrived. The saloonkeeper limped over to his table and sat down.

"You're an early riser," he smiled. "I just tumbled out of the bed roll. A bite to eat and then I'll clean up and shave before getting to work."

Slade nodded. Farr's lean cheeks were covered with a black stubble. Slade reflected that a few days without shaving and he would be able to boast a quite respectable beard. He also reflected on the psychological effect of suggestion. Had it not been Sliver Oakes' remark anent the ability of some men to grow whiskers quickly, he doubtless would hardly have noticed the hair on Farr's face.

"You'll be around at midnight?" Farr asked.

"I'll be here," Slade promised.

"The boys who take over this evening usually have a little game over at the corner table there," Farr said with a gesture to the other side of the dance floor. "Small stakes, just to while away the time. They'll be glad to have you join them if you care to."

He hesitated a moment, eyeing Slade. "I'll advance you a week's wages if you happen to be short," he said.

"Thanks, but I have a few pesos stowed away,"

Slade replied; "and I think I'll take a little ride this afternoon," he added.

Farr nodded his understanding. "My way of getting away from things, too," he said. "I'll just start off headed for nowhere and forget everything. When you're sort of born to a saddle there's no place like it to rest a man and clear his brain of cobwebs."

"You've been a cowhand?" Slade asked.

Farr gestured to his left leg. "That's how I got this short pin," he said. "Stampede, with me under it. Bone smashed all to heck. Doctors removed a chunk and managed to get the ends to knit, but it left me with a bad limp, as you may have noticed. All right in the saddle but slows up considerable on the ground. Had to give up range work. Went to work in a saloon over in New Mexico. Saw there was money to be made in the liquor business, and I had to do something to make a living. Had a few pesos laid aside. Managed to borrow some more and set up in business here. Place was pretty well run down and the man who owned it was glad to sell. I gambled on the town growing, and I was right, but I didn't figure it to boom like it did. Two years ago came the gold strikes and the town really began to hump itself. Yes, it grew, but not altogether the way I'd been hoping. We get a rough crowd here. They come from all over. The miners aren't exactly tame and a lot of them patronize the Branding

Pen. Same goes for the cowhands from the spreads to the east and north. But it's hellions like the Cholla Raiders who cause the real trouble. They seem to have connections everywhere, and they're deadly. I have rows in here every now and then, that's to be expected, but there have only been three killings here since I opened up, which is a better average than the Hog Waller and the Deuces-Up can brag about. And as I mentioned last night, all those killed happened to be floor men here. But somehow I've a notion there won't be any more."

"Hope you're right," Slade remarked cheerfully.

"I think I am," said Farr.

"Speaking of the other saloons, how about the Cattlemen's Club?" Slade asked.

"A quiet, well-appointed place," replied Farr. "Patronized mostly by the mine officials, foremen, spread owners and the older riders. Hunter keeps it orderly, but they did have a shooting in there a couple of months back that was a lulu. Nobody seemed able to say just how it started or what about, but when the smoke cleared there were four dead men on the floor and a bunch of half a dozen or so hellions went out the door in a flying wedge, forked their broncs and skalley-hooted. Happened so fast and so efficiently that it looks to me like it was a carefully planned job."

"Who were the men killed, local citizens?" Slade asked.

"They were not," Farr replied. "Nobody knew them, but they were hard-looking characters; the outlaw brand or I miss my guess."

Slade nodded. He was instantly of the opinion that the fight, or rather the execution, was the result of one outlaw bunch trying to horn in on another, but he didn't tell Farr so.

"Well," said Farr, rising to his feet, "I'm going to get cleaned up. See you tonight." He limped away. Slade watched him go, his eyes thoughtful. A moment later he pinched out his cigarette, and also left the saloon. Returning to the stable, he got the rig on Shadow and rode southwest toward the mouth of Dry Water Canyon.

EIGHT

The trail Slade followed from town was broad and deeply rutted by the wheels of heavily loaded wagons. Several times he pulled aside to let the great ore wagons pass on their way from the mine to the stamp mills on the outskirts of Cholla, where plenty of water was available; there was no water in the canyon.

Even in the bright sunlight of early afternoon, the mouth of Dry Water Canyon was gloomy. The perpendicular walls of darkly gray stone towered upward without a break for a good three hundred feet, their beetling crests overhanging. Along the base of the cliffs on either side were heavy banks of chaparral growth, but most of the floor was barren, studded with boulders and chimney rocks. Only gold, Slade reflected, could tempt men to enter such a dreary hole.

One other thing, however, might prove tempting to a certain brand of individual. The canyon was the most direct route to Mexico and the bleak mountains beyond. He thought of the mysterious band of horsemen he saw just as the dawn was breaking. Quite likely they were headed for *Mañana* Land after some foray.

Slade had covered something like two miles when, on rounding a shallow bend, he came upon a scene of activity in marked contrast to the silence and desolation he had just traversed. Men moved about briskly, winding engines chattered, ore rattled and thudded from the loading chutes to the beds of waiting wagons, tall stacks belched smoke, steam hissed. Everywhere was bustle and what looked to be utter confusion but was in fact orderly. It was the mouth of the Comstock mine.

Pulling Shadow to a halt, Slade hooked one long leg over the saddle horn, rolled a cigarette and sat surveying the activity with interest. In the face of the cliff was a dark opening, wide and high, the tunnel that bored into the hills, from which shafts descended to the various drifts or galleries of the Comstock. Branches of the tunnel also followed the veins of ore, and far down in the depths of the earth were other tunnels that tortured through the eternal stone.

A squat, ungainly figure disengaged from one of the groups and stumped along to where Slade sat his tall horse. It was old John Mosby, owner of the Comstock. He waved a greeting and paused beside Shadow's shoulder.

"Howdy?" he said. "Name's Slade, isn't it?"

"That's right," Slade smiled. "And I gather you are Mr. Mosby?"

"That's right, too," said old John. "Heard about you last night—heard you did a mighty good chore in the Branding Pen. Two of 'em, in fact. Bustin' Park Crony's hand for him sort of took

81

that quarrelsome hellion down a peg. Crony's a good worker and a good mining man, but he just can't behave himself when he's had a few drinks. Just naturally a good deal of a bully, because of his size and the way he can handle a shootin' iron. He needed the lesson he got. I've a notion he'll be a mite subdued for a while now. Light off and join me in a sandwich and a cup of coffee; was just going to have a snack. Come along, the cook shanty is right over there."

Slade liked Mosby's looks and accepted, snapping the bit from Shadow's mouth and loosening the cinches so the horse could graze in comfort on the sparse grass. Together they repaired to the cook shanty where a smiling Mexican cook set out enough appetizing provender for a round-up.

"Dig in," said Mosby, helping himself hugely. "Nobody can turn down Felipe's cooking, even if he has et breakfast just a little while before."

After sampling the offering, Slade agreed and made a very respectable second breakfast.

"You have a nice layout here, Mr. Mosby," he remarked as he pushed back his plate and reached for the makin's.

"Not bad, not bad," nodded Mosby. He twinkled his shrewd old eyes at the Ranger. "Not bad from a rabbit's foot."

"How's that?" Slade asked.

"I'll tell you about it," chuckled the mine owner.

"I started out as a cowhand but finally got tired of following a cow's tail for wages and decided to take a try at prospecting. Became a good deal of a desert rat, but did pretty well on the average. Worked over in this direction. Fellers had been picking up float and digging out pockets of little nuggets in the Cholla Hills for years. Decided to give them a whirl. In Harding I met Howard Hunter, who was a mining man and had just come down from the north. I told him about the Chollas and he got interested. Said the float and the pockets meant that somewhere in the hills were ledges from which they had been washed down. He said that in those ledges would be the big money. I figured he was right."

Mosby paused to light his pipe. When it was going to his satisfaction, he continued his story.

"So Hunter and me made up our minds to comb the Chollas proper. We worked up the west end of the hills and didn't have any luck. Came to Cholla, which wasn't much of a town in those days, and stayed there a couple of days to rest up. Then we headed south again, planning to split up and work the east side of the hills. Coming down from town and just to the north of the canyon you may have noticed a big dry wash that winds into the hills. Right where that wash begins we kicked up a rabbit that scooted out of the brush and hightailed into the canyon.

" 'There's a sign, Hunter,' I said. 'Rabbits are

lucky. You'd better follow the luck and go that way.'

" 'That's just superstition,' he said. 'I like the looks of the wash.' Well, he turned and went up the wash. Soon began picking up float and rooting out a few nuggets. And right after the last nugget he picked up he came upon a ledge that looked good. It was good. Right there he located the Last Nugget mine, which has been fair to middling and has made him considerable money. Nothing in the line of big medicine, but not bad."

Again Mosby twinkled at Slade.

"And what did you do?" El Halcon asked.

"I followed that jackrabbit with the lucky hind foot, and located the Comstock.

"Took Hunter quite a spell to get over it," Mosby added. "Took it in good part, though and admitted I gave him first choice. He did a lot of prospecting around in the lower canyon, trying to locate another Comstock, but didn't. Finally settled down to his own holding, opened the Cattlemen's Club in Cholla and has been doing pretty well there. I bought the Swinging J ranch against the day when the veins may peter out. Guess neither one of us has over much to complain of. I'm doing all right and would do a lot better if some sidewinders weren't stealing me blind."

"Yes?" Slade prompted casually.

Old John's face darkened. "My highgrade ore," he explained. "The veins are spotty with pockets of highgrade, and it's the highgrade that makes the Comstock pay. Without it I could hardly meet expenses. It's rich, but a lot of that highgrade never reaches my mill. I have a big working here, employ nearly four hundred men, and you can't keep tabs on everybody. But how they get it out of the mine without being caught up is beyond me, but they do."

"Any other mines nearby into which they might be able to slip it?" Slade asked.

"None within several miles to the north and east," Mosby replied. "You can't run a tunnel several miles without attracting attention."

"Hardly," Slade admitted.

"Anyhow, somebody is widelooping it," growled Mosby. "For the past six months the highgrade has been showing mighty scarce at the mills. I *know* it's still coming out of the veins. There's no way to tell when the highgrade pockets are going to show, but they wouldn't peter out all of a sudden with the veins still running along average. I suppose the blasted Cholla Raiders have something to do with it, but I sure couldn't prove it, even if I knew who the devil they are to prove it against."

"Would be an unusual owlhoot band to go in for something like that," Slade commented.

"Oh, they're unusual all right," grunted Mosby.

"A mighty smart man handling 'em." He glanced around, saw that the cook was not nearby, and lowered his voice.

"Sheriff Cole has a considerable notion that Carry Farr might be at the head of the outfit," he said. "Could be, but I personally don't think Farr has that kind of brains."

Slade nodded, but did not otherwise comment.

"Well, got to get back on the job," Mosby said. "Drop around any time you are of a mind to. You're nice to talk with.

"Only," he added in a mutter after Slade had ridden off, "you sure don't do any talking. Didn't tell me a darn thing about yourself, even when I figured I was sounding you out. And I got a notion you pumped me dry without me catching on."

Which, had Mosby known it, was exactly in line with what other men had complained about Walt Slade.

Leaving the site of the mine, Slade rode on down the narrow canyon. Soon the floor, which heretofore had been quite level, developed a downward slant. So steep that Shadow picked his way gingerly over the small boulders and bits of talus. Deeper and deeper became the gorge, with a corresponding heightening of the sheer walls. The nature of the cliffs had changed, the dusty gray of the quartz being replaced by a reddish granite curiously striated.

"Horse, there was a great subsidence here,

perhaps a few million years ago," Slade remarked to Shadow.

Shortly before the death of his father, subsequent to business reverses which entailed the loss of the elder Slade's ranch, young Walt had graduated from a famous college of engineering. He had planned to take a post-grad course in special subjects to round out his education. That became impossible for the time being and when Captain Jim McNelty, commander of the famous Border Battalion of the Texas Rangers, with whom Slade had worked some during summer vacations, suggested that he come into the Rangers and continue his studies in spare time, Slade thought it a good idea. Long since he had gotten from private study as much and more than he could have hoped to acquire from the postgrad. He was amply prepared to enter the profession he had thought to make his life's work.

But Ranger work had gotten a strong hold on him and he was loth to sever connections with the illustrious body of law enforcement officers. He was young and there was plenty of time to become an engineer. He'd stick with the Rangers for a while.

Incidentally, his engineering knowledge had more than once proven valuable in the course of his Ranger activities. Now he surveyed the unusual formation with the eye of a geologist.

"Yes, a great subsidence," he repeated. "During

some convulsion of nature, the canyon floor dropped hundreds of feet to its present level. Interesting."

Finally the floor levelled off again, and now the great ruddy ribs of rock which hemmed it in soared upward for more than a thousand feet. Slate estimated that the floor was between five and six hundred feet lower than it was at the site of the Comstock mine. It had become almost naked rock save along the base of the cliffs, where a shallow belt of growth was tall, thorny and thick. Slade eyed the terrain ahead and uttered an exclamation.

"And a lot of water came down here once upon a time," he told Shadow. "But where in blazes did it come from? Not from the upper canyon, and certainly not over the cliffs. Big springs here once, I suppose. Were buried in the course of the disturbance which dropped the canyon floor and gradually, perhaps over a period of many years, caused the springs to dry up."

As he rode down the canyon, Slade had continually scanned the ground for signs of horses recently passing that way; there were plenty of indications that they had. Here on the bare stone their irons had of course left no marks other than an occasional shod hoof scratch. Where he was riding at the moment were quite a few scrapings, as if the animals had been pulled to a halt and allowed to stand for some time. He rode on and after a few hundred yards abruptly pulled Shadow to a halt. Directly ahead the floor of the canyon had changed to soft earth. The dirt was scarred by the marks of hoofs, but none of them fresh. Slade estimated that none could be less than a couple of weeks old. The edges were sloughed off by rain which had fallen several days before and there was a swelling of caked mud in the indentations, where water had stood. Why did the mysterious night riders come just so far and stop? he wondered. To make sure he was not mistaken, he rode backward and forward across the canyon, scanning the surface with eyes that missed nothing.

Then suddenly he saw something that puzzled him even more. Among the horses' hoof prints were the narrower tracks of shod mules, and he was confident he would have spotted mule tracks on his way down the canyon, had there been any. Where had the long-eared critters come from, and why? Could have come up the canyon, of course, but why, like the horses traveling in the other direction, had they stopped at this point? Slade's Ranger training had taught him never to overlook or discard anything that was out of the ordinary, and this certainly was, although he had not the slightest notion what it could mean. With a shake of his head, he rode on.

The contours of the canyon were changing, the walls greatly lessened in height and split by fissures and narrow gorges. The floor was again hard and stony, the tracks left by the passing animals so nearly obliterated that in the deepening gloom he gave up trying to trace them. The horses and mules could turn off into any of the side canyons without leaving evidence that they had done so. He glanced at the western sky, slowed Shadow and turned his head.

"Time we were getting back to town," he told the cayuse. "Sift sand!"

Shadow set off on the return trip at a good pace, but twilight was falling when he passed the site of the Comstock mine. Slade continually scanned the surrounding terrain with a carping gaze.

In men who ride much alone with danger as a stirrup companion there develops a subtle sixth sense that warns of peril when none, so far as can be noted, is present. And now for no good reason, apparently, Slade had become acutely uneasy. Far ahead a belt of thicket, dark, immutable, edged close to the trail. The Ranger all of a sudden didn't want to pass that shadowy mass of growth with the dying light in the west striking full upon him. He hesitated, tempted not to give way to what appeared to be an absurd premonition; but the warning monitor in his brain continued its voiceless clamor. Grinning a little sheepishly, he left the trail and sent his horse straight across the canyon, not turning his head north again until he was riding in the shadow of the growth that flanked the canyon wall, never taking his eyes from the belt of thicket which now drew steadily nearer but nearly two hundred yards east of where he paced his horse.

Abruptly he noticed something that intensified his interest. Several birds were fluttering about over the thicket, which was doubtless their sleeping place, apparently reluctant to settle in the branches. The concentration furrow deepened between Slade's black brows. He pulled Shadow to a halt and studied the growth over which the birds dipped and wheeled. Between the thicket and where he sat his horse were small clumps of chaparral and several large boulders. Making up his mind to a course of action, he swung from the saddle and dropped the split reins to the ground.

"Stay put," he told Shadow, "I'm going to see if there's something holed up in that brush heap. Could be only a snake on a limb, or a bobcat, but it could be something else, from the way those feathered gents are acting."

It was a ticklish chore which Slade had set for himself. There were open spaces between the clumps of brush and the boulders, with still enough light for accurate shooting. He banked on the drygulcher, if there was one in the thicket, keeping his eyes fixed on the trail; but the slightest sound could well cause him to turn and inspect the ground behind the thicket. And there was always the chance that the possible watcher had seen him turn from the trail and anticipated just such a move as he was making. Slade thought this unlikely, however, a slight nearby rise in the trail probably obscuring the view of the distant trail to a man low down amid the growth.

Nevertheless, he glided forward with the greatest caution, peering, listening, remained concealed for moments behind each sheltering bunch of growth. Once his scalp prickled as he stepped on a dry stick that broke under his foot with a soft little crack which sounded unduly loud in the great stillness of the evening. A vivid imagination pictured the unseen watcher swinging around, peering through the screen of growth, his gun muzzle lining with the figure crouched behind a deplorably scanty clump of bush.

However, nothing happened, and after a period of waiting for his nerves to quiet down, he pursued his hazardous course. Nearer and nearer to the shadowy thicket he drew, slowing his pace, increasing his vigilance. Now he was where he could not see the birds over the far side of the growth, which might warn him of any sudden activity behind the bristle of gnarled mesquite. He drew a deep breath of relief as he reached the growth and glided into it; now, if something cut loose, it would be on more even terms. Foot by slow foot he inched along, listening for the slightest sound, watchful for any sudden movement. Abruptly he froze to immobility. He was almost to the outer fringe of growth and directly in front of him was a denser block of shadow that resolved into a man crouching behind a straggle of bush and peering intently down the trail. Slade could make out the gleam of the rifle barrel held at the ready. No doubt but the devil was there to do murder. Again he stole forward; could he take the fellow alive, he might be able to wring valuable information from him. So intent was he on the crouching quarry that he neglected to be careful where he placed his feet. He kicked a loose stone that slammed against another with a ringing crack.

The crouching figure whirled, flinging up the rifle. Slade drew and shot, the two reports blending almost as one. A slug whined past his ear so close he felt the breath of its passing. The figure in the brush reeled back with a yell; the rifle fell to the ground. But before Slade could line sights again in the illusive dusk, the fellow dived into the thicker growth. Slade bounded forward, a trailing vine caught his ankle and he fell heavily.

Before he could disentangle himself from the vine and scramble to his feet, he heard the explosive snort of a spurred horse and a drumming of fast hoofs fading away into the north. When he reached the outer fringe of growth, the fellow was but a brown smudge on the gray trail and out of six-gun range. Slade watched him vanish into the deeper dark, then turned and made his way back through the brush. He located the fallen rifle and tucked it under his arm after a brief examination. It was a good weapon, almost new, with nothing about it to distinguish it from any other of the same make and caliber. He'd present it to Sliver Oakes, without any explanation.

"No sense in trying to run down the side-winder," he told Shadow as he swung into the saddle. "He's got a head start and would reach town before we could catch him up. Easy for him to slide into hiding there. I think he got something to remember us by, judging from the way he yelped. Too dark to see if there were any blood spots on the leaves, but I'm pretty sure he felt lead. Nothing much, though, the chances are. Sure didn't slow him down any. If I'd just watched where I was going and hadn't kicked that infernal rock I'd have had a good chance to grab him, but I bungled it.

"Oh, well," he added philosophically, "guess most folks do more foolish things than wise ones; but I sometimes think I'm exceptionally cursed in that respect." He headed for town in a disgruntled frame of mind.

NINE

As he rode, Slade pondered what without doubt had been an intended attempt on his life. And which, had he not followed a hunch based on his presentiment of impending danger, would quite likely have been successful. Appeared his every move was watched, or anticipated. Nobody other than Sliver Oakes and Carry Farr knew he intended to take a ride, and he had not confided to even them that he planned to ride down Dry Water Canyon.

But somebody had either known or had divined his intention. Presumably somebody in Cholla, although his short stay at the Comstock mine might have been noted and taken advantage of by somebody there. Either way, it behooved him to walk warily. Somebody was out to get him. Whether because of his brush with the outlaws on the trail just south of Harding or because of El Halcon's reputation for horning in on good things others had started, he had no way of knowing. Anyhow, in certain quarters he was considered a menace that must, if possible, he eliminated. He did not believe that his Ranger connection was known, although that was not to be altogether discounted. However, he considered the possibility very slight. The attempted drygulching ruled against it. Even the saltiest outlaw bunch would hesitate at murdering a Texas Ranger. The slain man would instantly be replaced, quite likely by a number of the grim "Gentlemen in the White Hats" who would never give up the quest and would eventually wreak a terrible vengeance on all responsible for the killing. But El Halcon, believed by many to be just a smart owlhoot, was a horse with different stripes down its back. El Halcon would be fair game, with quite a few folks considering that somebody finally did a good chore.

Which was why Captain McNelty had more than once protested Slade's allowing El Halcon's dubious reputation to grow.

"But it opens up avenues of information that would be closed to a known peace officer," Slade would point out; and Captain Jim, albeit reluctantly and with a doubtful mind, would still his objections.

"The ablest and most fearless Ranger of them all," said those who knew the truth. "A blasted slick-ironer if there ever was one!" said many who saw only El Halcon.

After stabling his horse, Slade repaired to the Branding Pen for something to eat before going to work. It wanted a couple hours of midnight, but he welcomed a chance to study the crowd a bit at his leisure.

Carry Farr limped over to his table and sat

down. "Busy night," he observed. "You may have your hands full."

"Possibly," Slade agreed, taking a sip of coffee.

"But I think you'll be able to take care of anything that comes your way," Farr added. "Watch the games close. As I said, I try to run straight games, and I'm sure you can help me."

With a nod, he shambled off. Slade finished his meal, enjoyed a cigarette and ran his eyes over the gathering. A rough crowd, all right, but for the most part not bad. He did not anticipate any real trouble with the customers, but he quickly arrived at the conclusion that the dealers would bear watching. As was common in such places, they played their hands, and passed the deal if requested to do so, which was not often, because it slowed up the game. Finally he rose to his feet, sauntered over to where the day man sat on his high stool, a sawed-off shotgun cradled over his knees.

"Okay," Slade told him, "I'm taking over."

Thus amid the frankly lawless element, the reckless cowboys, and the trouble-hunting miners who frequented the Branding Pen, Walt Slade took up his new duties peacefully and serenely. Unlike his predecessors, who were now riding herd on the Milky Way, perhaps, he dispensed with the high "lookout chair" and the clumsy shotgun. Lithe, alert, he mingled with the crowd, seeing everything while apparently paying scant attention to anything. Before long he observed a dealer making a deck change spots and color, getting himself a little private cut.

Slade had a waiter call the dealer aside. Quietly he told him what he had seen and suggested that he cut it out. The dealer, a big man with a hard jaw and truculent eyes, glowered at Slade and his face flushed darkly.

"I know my business," he spat, "and I don't need no blasted lookout to tell it to me."

One fifteenth of a second later he sat down on the floor, and sat down hard. Slade took him by the collar and the seat of the pants and threw him through a window, without waiting to open said window. The gambler "opened" it on his way out.

He came back by way of the door, streaming blood from a score of cuts, a gun in one hand and a knife in the other. Slade shot the gun from his hand, took the knife away from him and sent him out again, via the window. He stayed out.

The bit of byplay was "noticed" by the other dealers and some professional gamblers who frequented the place. Within a few days the word got around that the games at the Branding Pen were straight without reservation. As a result, business improved.

"Why there's even fellers who used to go no place but Hunter's Cattlemen's Club sitting in our games now," chuckled Carry Farr. "And look at old man Ward of the C Bar Q bucking the wheel over there. He'll toss away the price of fifty prime beef critters in an evening and think nothing of it. Take a busted nickel off him crooked and he'll shoot out the lights!"

Thus an uneventful week passed. There were a few friendly cuttings and shootings in the Hog Waller and the Deuces-Up, nothing serious. One gentleman was slightly ventilated in the Cattlemen's Club. Such things were to be expected. But not even such minor incidents disturbed the tranquility of the Branding Pen.

Sliver Oakes snorted at the stories which came his way.

"Yep, you're getting a reputation, all right," he squeaked to Slade. "And," he added darkly, "that's just what'll be your finish. Salty jiggers are going to hear about you and set out to get themselves a reputation by downing you. Just pay mind to what I tell you and see if I ain't right."

Slade smiled down at the plump pessimist from his great height, and did not take the trouble to contradict him.

Carry Farr was greatly pleased with his acquisition and said so in no uncertain terms.

Walt Slade, though, was not pleased with the way things were going. Captain McNelty didn't send him to Cholla to prosper Carry Farr's business but to ferret out and apprehend certain lawbreakers, and so far Slade felt he had not made the slightest progress. He didn't know who to suspect or where to look for the perpetrators of the atrocities which had disturbed the section. He could sympathize with Sheriff Cole.

Sliver Oakes' perverted sense of humor seemed to enjoy the sheriff's frustration.

"He's pawin' sod like a tail-twisted shorthorn, but it won't do him no good," Sliver chuckled apropos of the impotent peace officer. "The Cholla Raiders have sure got him buffaloed. Spends nearly all his time here. Even opened up a branch office. Things are always plumb peaceful over at the county seat, so he left a fat old deputy in charge there and practically moved to Cholla. Half the time I figure he don't know which end is up. Neither one is any good against the Raiders. And John Mosby keeps bellerin' that he's losing more highgrade, and 'lows the Raiders are to blame, though how he figures that is beyond me. By the way, they've been mighty quiet since the stage robbery up by Harding. Maybe you coming into the section has scared 'em."

"I doubt it," Slade replied. "If what you tell of them is correct, they're not the sort to scare easy. Chances are they're just waiting for something worthwhile to come their way; then they'll cut loose again."

"Wouldn't be surprised if you're right," Sliver agreed soberly.

That night when Slade showed up at the Branding Pen for work, Carry Farr was not around and Cook, the head bartender, was in charge.

"He rode off early this morning," explained Cook. "Said he needed to get the smoke outa his lungs. May come in tonight, may be gone a week. You never can tell about him when he ambles off on one of those jaunts. He said to tell you to go right ahead with whatever you think best. Looks like a big night, doesn't it?"

Slade nodded absently; his thoughts were elsewhere. Must have been a sudden decision on Farr's part; he had not hinted of any such intention at five o'clock in the morning when Slade told him goodnight.

Three days later, an urgent message came over the wire from Harding to Sheriff Cole:

SUNRISE LIMITED WRECKED. EXPRESS MESSENGER KILLED. TEN THOUSAND DOLLARS TAKEN FROM EXPRESS CAR.

Slade watched Sheriff Cole and his posse tear out of town, and shook his head. There was no doubt in his mind but that the sheriff was off on another wild goose chase.

That night, Slade was silent and preoccupied, going about his work in a mechanical fashion. He was glad that it was a dull night, for he was busy with his thoughts. His hunch had been a straight one when he expressed the opinion to Sliver Oakes that the Raiders were just biding their time, waiting for something worth their while before they staged another foray. And what the devil to do about it!

Suddenly a thought struck him. He glanced at the clock over the bar; the hands stood at four in the morning. He sought out Cook, who was having a snack at one of the tables.

"If you don't mind, I think I'll knock off a mite early tonight," he told the bartender. "Things are quiet and you shouldn't have any trouble."

"Go right ahead," replied Cook. "I'll take care of everything and close up; won't be anybody here in another hour."

At the livery stable, Slade swiftly got the rig on Shadow. Five minutes later found him heading down Dry Water Canyon at a fast pace. Alert and watchful he rode, his eyes constantly ranging ahead to the extent of his vision, his ears attuned to every sound that broke the silence. Mile after mile he rode without drawing rein, between the ever-heightening walls, deep into the lower fastnesses of Dry Water Canyon.

The dawn broke in primrose and gold. The bare blue bones of the mountains showed between tresses of fleecy cloud. The wind blew clear and clean for wide, unhindered miles down the gorge. The tall sky smiled on the silken sheen of the grasses. Trees and bushes wore feathers of green that flaunted their wavering beauty in the rushing air. Despite the problems that beset him, Walt

Slade felt it was good to be alive on such a morning.

"With so much loveliness all about them, it would seem that men would absorb something of the cleanness of the wind, the gladness of the sun and the peace of the mountains," he observed to Shadow. "Doesn't appear to be so in lots of cases, though. They treasure muck and forget the heights. June along, horse, we've got things to do."

When he reached the long stretch of almost naked rock that was the canyon floor, Slade slowed Shadow. His eyes roved about seeking something that continued to elude him. Finally he pulled to a halt where the rock so abruptly changed to soft earth.

"A straight hunch, horse, though what it'll get us I don't know," he remarked aloud.

It had rained the night before and the earthen floor ahead was soft and spongy; and scoring its surface were the prints of horses, coming south, and, Slade could see, only a few hours old. Made, he felt sure, by the mounts of the band that robbed the Sunrise Limited. As he had suspected, Dry Water Canyon was their get-away route, into which they circled from the north. With the sheriff and his posse scouring the hills to the west and south of Harding, the obvious road to the Mexican Border.

But where the devil did they go? Very likely, he

thought, they continued south and slid into Cholla by twos and threes and holed up there. If so, it seemed that he should have met them on his way down the canyon. Which might not have been in his favor.

Turning Shadow, he rode back up the canyon, slowly, scanning every foot of the ground with the greatest care. And gradually, to his utter bewilderment, he became convinced that no troop of horsemen had passed that way within the past thirty-six hours. But where the devil did the hellions get to? He pulled to a halt and stared at the sheer cliffs which seemed to mock him. The twigs of the growth flanking their base winked derisively in the sunlight.

Could they have holed up in the brush? Slade shook his head. The belt of growth was too narrow to provide concealment for a dozen riders and their mounts. No, that was out. Completely nonplussed, he headed back to town, turning the perplexing problem over in his mind, exploring every angle, and getting exactly nowhere. He passed the busy site of the Comstock mine and rode on, more than usually alert. Nothing untoward happened, however, and he reached Cholla about midafternoon and immediately went to bed.

Slade slept until well after dark, and when he awakened, Sliver Oakes had news for him.

"Sheriff got back just a little while ago," said

Sliver. "Didn't have no luck, per usual. Tracked the hellions into the hills, then lost 'em. They loosened a couple of rails on a curve and put the Limited in the ditch. Nobody bad hurt except the express messenger, who was killed by the dynamite explosion when they blew the express car door."

"Blew the safe, too, I suppose," Slade commented.

"Nope," replied Sliver, "They drilled out the combination knob. Conductor said it was a plumb professional job, didn't take 'em fifteen minutes. The bunch held the trainmen and the passengers in the coaches while a feller with black whiskers got off his horse through the car door and with another jigger worked on the safe. Packed out ten thousand dollars, nearly, in bills and coin. The big jigger crawled on his horse from the door and away they went, hell bent for leather. Whole job didn't take more 'n half an hour, according to folks on the train. Brakeman climbed a pole and cut in a portable telegraph instrument and they notified Harding in a jiffy. Not that it did any good except to get the wreck train there fast. Hellions were done gone."

"Drilled the safe," Slade repeated thoughtfully. "That's unusual for this section of the country."

"Everything about those blasted Cholla Raiders is unusual," Sliver replied sententiously. Slade did not argue the point.

Slade was eating his evening meal in the Branding Pen when Carry Farr limped in. He was dusty and travel stained, with a black stubble on his cheeks and chin, but his eyes were bright and he looked cheerful and rested.

"Nothing like a good long ride to set you up," he said as he dropped in a chair. "Anything happen while I was gone?"

"Nothing here," Slade answered, and proceeded to regale him with an account of the train robbery, closely watching Farr's reactions the while.

The saloonkeeper listened intently, clucking in his throat from time to time as the tale progressed.

"An efficient bunch, all right," was his comment when Slade paused. "Yes, they sure knew their business. Don't suppose anybody got a good look at them?"

"I understand they were masked," Slade replied. Farr nodded.

"Which means, I'd say, that the hellions show up in the towns hereabout. Yes, a local outfit, all right, with a plumb smart man at the top. No brushpoppin' outfit, that. But where the devil do they hole up? Chances are the sidewinders are right here in town by now, but they must have a headquarters somewhere to work from, and it wouldn't be here. Of course those blasted Cholla Hills are full of cracks and holes, with trails leading to them for those who know them. But it's strange that an old-timer in the section like

Sheriff Cole can't ferret them out. Suppose he'll be around after a while asking me some questions. He's pretty well convinced that I'm tied up with the bunch or know who they are. Well, let him come. When you have a clear conscience, you don't need to worry."

He beckoned a waiter and ordered a bountiful meal. "Was way over to Marathon," he remarked as he settled down to his food. "Know the town marshal there, feller named Whetsell; we had quite a gabfest. We used to work for the same spread, the Triangle Dot. I was telling him about you and the way Sheriff Cole looked at you sideways. He seemed to find it funny, for he chuckled and chuckled again. I couldn't see anything amusing about it."

Slade nodded and rose to his feet. "About time for me to relieve Pete," he said. Farr also nodded and went on eating.

Walt Slade went to bed in the wee hours of the morning in anything but a complacent frame of mind. It seemed that anything which looked like a promising lead insisted on petering out.

He knew the town marshal at Marathon, and the marshal knew him and all about him, and his name *was* Whetsell.

TEN

When Slade repaired to the Branding Pen for his breakfast, around noon, he found Carry Farr in a restless mood.

"What you say we take a walk around the town?" the saloonkeeper suggested. "Sometimes I think I don't do enough of it; would be better for this game leg of mine, the chances are, if I walked more."

Slade offered no objections and they set out. As they strolled about, Slade pondered the booming, bustling town of Cholla, what it had been and no doubt what it would be again. It reminded Slade of certain ghost towns he had seen in the Tuolumne Valley in California. Just a cabin or two, a few decayed and broken walls, a tottery chimney were all that were to be seen over the wide expanse of hill and forest. Yet a flourishing city of two or three thousand population had occupied the grassy dead solitude during flush mining times perhaps a dozen years before, and the lonely cabins had been the center of the teeming hive, the heart of the little city. Then the mines gave out, the town fell into decay and in a few years wholly disappeared— streets, dwellings, shops, everything. A few pocket miners occupied the cabins. They had seen the town spring up, spread, grow, flourish in its pride; and they had seen it sicken and die, and pass away like a dream. There were many such dotting the hills and valleys of the West. Very likely it would be the same with Cholla when the gold veins finally petered out. Cholla had been a lonely supply depot for the neighborhood ranches, but the spreads would turn to Harding on the railroad and Cholla would become but a memory.

They passed the gaunt buildings on the edge of town which housed the stamp mills where the ponderous iron pestles quivered the air with their ceaseless dance that ground the gold ore to powder from which the precious metal would be retrieved by the amalgam method and cast into ingots.

Circling around through the outskirts of the town, they reached the foot of Main Street and sauntered up the busy thoroughfare, pausing to glance into shop windows, discussing the varied merchandise displayed.

"The Hog Waller," said Farr, jerking his thumb toward a broad expanse of plate glass window. "Mostly patronized by the cowhands from the spreads to the east. Couple of blocks farther along is the Deuces-Up, gets nearly all miners. Across the street is Hunter's Cattlemen's Club, gets the higher brackets. The Branding Pen gets everything."

Four blocks east of the Branding Pen, on a corner, was a squat, strongly constructed building with barred windows and a massive front door. It was the Cholla bank. A mule cart guarded by two watchful individuals with sawed-off shotguns stood at the curb. From it men were carrying ingots of metal into the bank. The ingots were evidently surprisingly heavy for their size.

"It's the monthly clean-up of the Last Nugget, Hunter's mine," explained Farr, who recognized the cart and its driver. "Couple of months' clean-up, for that matter. The hellions who robbed the Harding stage missed the Last Nugget's big shipment. Hunter had only a little one in that batch, comparatively speaking, but the Comstock's was a whopper."

Slade eyed the ingots curiously. "How many mines does Hunter own?" he asked.

"Just the Last Nugget," Farr replied. "It's a pretty good lode, but not up to the Comstock by a long ways. Hunter's making money above operating expenses, which are heavy, but John Mosby is getting rich from the Comstock, or was before he began losing so much highgrade ore."

Slade continued to gaze at the ingots, the concentration furrow deep between his black brows.

"And Hunter operates just the one mine," he remarked, almost to himself.

"That's right," said Farr. "Hello, here comes the sheriff. Howdy, Wes?" he greeted as the sheriff paused beside the cart.

The sheriff acknowledged the greeting with a stiff jerk of his head. His choleric old eyes went over Slade from head to foot. El Halcon's amused gaze, which met his suspicious glare unwaveringly, plainly irked the sheriff.

"Why *did* you have to squat here?" he demanded. "Didn't I say you're a bad luck piece and that trouble just follows you around and busts loose all over the place wherever you happen to be? And of all places, why'd you have to go to work in that rumhole up the street?"

Slade's eyes danced and the corners of his mouth quirked upward. He countered the sheriff's interrogative volley with a question of his own.

"Where are the other twelve gents?"

The sheriff blinked and stared. "What? What the devil?" he sputtered in bewildered tones.

"You see, it's this way," Slade explained confidentially, "the last time I was asked a lot of questions there were twelve men sitting alongside in a box listening."

The sheriff blinked again. Then his blocky face turned fiery red as he got the meaning. He gurgled in his throat, snapped at his mustache and seemed about to explode. With a mighty effort he mastered his indignation, but his eyes remained red.

"You watch your step, you impudent whippersnapper, or it won't be the last time there's a jury listening to you answering questions," he fumed. "I've got my eye on you—on both of you hellions—and don't you forget it!"

He stormed into the bank in the wake of the

last ingot, still mumbling under his mustache. Slade watched him go with laughing eyes.

Carry Farr, however, was serious. "There's no sense in getting the old jigger all hopped up against you," he remonstrated. "No sense in going out of your way looking for trouble."

"Looking for trouble is sometimes the best way to avoid finding it," Slade replied enigmatically. Abruptly his face was serious as Farr's.

"Do you happen to know when the Comstock mine will send a shipment to the bank?" he asked.

"They should be running one down from the mill about this time tomorrow afternoon," Farr replied. "The bank usually sends a shipment to Harding on the first or the fifteenth, and day after tomorrow is the first of the month. Why?"

"I want to get a look at that shipment," Slade replied.

Farr cast him a questioning glance, but Slade offered no explanation. Farr grunted and "dotted" his way to the saloon in silence.

When they reached the Branding Pen, Farr jerked his head toward the back room. Slade nodded and followed him. Farr locked the door and they sat down at the table, after Farr had made sure the back door was also locked.

"Slade," the saloonkeeper said, "there's something I've wanted to bring up for some time, but I've sort of been waiting for you to mention it. Remember the first night you were here, when those gents with the shotgun barged in on us?"

"I'm not apt to forget it," Slade replied.

Farr leaned forward, his eyes hard on El Halcon's face. "And did you happen to notice that night that the bolt had been removed from the back door lock?" he asked softly.

"I did," Slade replied.

"And why didn't you mention it?"

"Because I didn't want to be the first to notice it," Slade answered ambiguously.

Farr looked bewildered. "And what do you mean by that?" he demanded.

"I mean," Slade replied, "that there was no doubt in my mind but that it was an inside job. The bolt could not have been removed from outside the door. Who found out it had been removed?"

"Cook, my head bartender."

"And what did he have to say about it?"

"A number of things that wouldn't look good in print," Farr answered with a fleeting grin.

"I believe you said Cook has a key to the door?"

"That's right."

"And does he always carry it in his pocket?"

"I imagine he keeps it in the till most of the time," Farr replied.

"Where anybody working here, say a swamper or one of the kitchen help, could easily get at it. I imagine you have something of a turnover in that type of employee?"

"Yes, we do change swampers and dishwashers

pretty often—they come and they go," admitted Farr. "But Cook would have missed the key if it were stolen."

"Would have been no necessity for stealing it," Slade answered. "Would take but a moment to get an impress on a bit of wax in the palm of the hand, or even a bit of soft soap. Anybody handy with a file could duplicate that kind of a key without any trouble."

"But if they had a duplicate key, why wouldn't they just use that to get in?" Farr asked.

"Because if you happened to leave your key in the lock inside, as it appears you have a habit of doing—it was in the lock that night and is right now—it would have been impossible to open the door with a key from the outside. Also, manipulating a key would be almost certain to make some noise. With the bolt removed, the door could be gently pushed open without a sound. Somebody with a duplicate key slipped in when there happened to be no key in the lock and removed the bolt, which could be done easily and quickly by anybody thoroughly familiar with locks. The door being seldom used as an exit, the absence of the bolt would very likely have not been noticed for some time."

"But, blazes!" exclaimed Farr. "Those two hellions were after you, and they couldn't possibly have known beforehand that you would be in here that night."

"My being here was just a coincidence that worked in with somebody's plan to get rid of me, which apparently was considered more important than the money in your safe, for there's little doubt but that robbery was what was originally in mind," Slade replied. "Remember one of the men who died here that night was seen drinking at the bar only a short time before. He saw us enter the back room, slid out and notified somebody with a hairtrigger brain who immediately saw opportunity and tried to take advantage of it.

"All of which goes to show just what the section is up against," Slade concluded. "Somebody with intelligence far above the average, who misses no bets."

Slade made it his business to be in the neighborhood of the bank the following afternoon when the Comstock clean-up was carried into the vault. He got a good look at the ingots, which he studied with lively interest. After which he made his way to his little room in the stable and sat for some time smoking and gazing out the window. There was a pleased glow in his eyes when he descended to commune a moment with Shadow.

"Horse, at last it's tying up," he told the big black. "Now I'm pretty sure as to who's doing it. All I've got to find out is *how* he does it.

"Which," he added reflectively, "appears to be a good deal of a chore."

ELEVEN

When Slade awoke the following morning Sliver Oakes, as usual, had some news for him.

"John Mosby and Hunter sure aren't taking any chances with that big shipment going to Harding tomorrow," said Sliver. "A guard inside the stage, one on top with the driver, and six outriders, all loaded for bear. Mosby swears this is one the Cholla riders ain't going to lay a finger on. Says he hopes they try it and get their comeuppance."

"I imagine they're too smart to buck such a layout," Slade observed.

"So I'd say, too, but you never can tell about those galoots," replied Sliver. "They might figure some smart trick and put it over. Bet their mouths are watering for that shipment. A big one. Nearly fifty thousand dollars' worth of metal. Worth taking a chance for. I've a notion it'll get through, though."

Slade nodded agreement, but his eyes were serious; such a potential haul would be a temptation to any owlhoot bunch, and the Raiders had shown themselves to be daring and resourceful. They *might* find a way. As he ate his breakfast, Slade tried to put himself in the position of the outlaws, to see with their eyes a possible flaw in the defense of the treasure which they might take advantage of. However, he could think of no possible way in which the robbers might circumvent the vigilance of the guards and outriders. And yet—

Suddenly his eyes glowed. He was thinking of the unusual technique employed in the robbery of the Sunrise Limited express car.

"They might try it," he told the salt shaker. "Hit when and where nobody expects them to. Yes, and they might well get away with it."

He finished his meal and glanced at the clock. Almost time to go to work. Carry Farr was at the far end of the bar by the till, his usual position. Slade sauntered over to him.

"I'd like to have a word with you in the back room," he told the saloonkeeper. Farr shot him a quick glance, then led the way to the back room without comment. They sat down at the table facing each other. There was a quizzical gleam in the depths of Farr's cold eyes, but he still said nothing.

Slade also sat silent for a moment, his gaze fixed on the one feature of the saloonkeeper's sinister-appearing face that had caused him from the first to have an open mind concerning Carry Farr.

It seemed to Walt Slade, old in experience with men—especially sinister men—despite his youthfulness of years, that Carry Farr's nose somewhat redeemed his unprepossessing face. It was a good straight nose, with something of the pleasant tiptiltedness of a child's. It was the kind of a nose, Slade thought, that should have been set above a grin-quirked mouth and between twinkling eyes. Which was decidedly not the case.

Just the same that beak might be something to catch onto and hold onto. He had a whimsical feeling that when the Big Boss of the Range Up Above did a real job, He usually left something He could reach down and get a good hold on, no matter how botched-up the job might appear at first look, and if there was something *real* inside a person it showed through to the outside, one way or another, if you looked close enough. Too many people didn't look close enough. His droll reflections caused his eyes to crinkle a little with inward laughter, and for the first time he saw laughter in Carry Farr's eyes. He couldn't suppress an answering grin.

"All right," he chuckled, "let's have it!"

Farr's chuckle was an echo of his own. "Finally decided I'm to be trusted, eh?" Farr said.

"Okay," Slade repeated, "let's have it."

Farr filled and lighted his pipe before replying. "Well," he said at length, "I have a knack of not forgetting faces, especially if I've seen 'em through powder smoke. Remember the big fight in front of the Holman bank when the Dotson boys tried to stick up the bank and a couple of Rangers had been tipped off to what was in the wind? I happened to be in Holman that day, in Buster's hardware store right across the street from the bank. I saw one of the Rangers down two of the Dotson brothers before they could clear leather. I got a good look at him and wasn't likely to forget him."

"You know how to keep a tight latigo on your jaw," Slade smiled admiringly.

"I figured when you were ready to give out information you'd do it," explained Farr. "Wasn't for me to be talking out of turn. So McNelty sent you here in answer to John Mosby's letter, eh? It leaked out somehow that John wrote the letter and got a sort of vague reply. He felt McNelty let him down."

"Captain Jim never lets anybody down," Slade said quietly. "He just decided that somebody whose Ranger connections might not be known in the section would possibly have better luck, that's all."

"So I gather," nodded Farr. "Sheriff Cole was sort of miffed by Mosby writing that letter, felt he was going over his head, but old John said something has got to be done and that Cole wasn't having any luck doing it. You had any luck?"

"I rather think so," Slade replied, "although so far I have no proof against anybody. Perhaps I'll be able to get some tonight, with your help."

"Anything I can do," Farr instantly promised. "Name it."

"I want you to extinguish the light and let me

slide out the back door to the alley," Slade replied. "Stick around and if I should happen to come back in a hurry, put out the light again and let me in when I knock."

"Think there's something in the wind?" Farr asked.

"I'm playing a hunch that there is," Slade replied. "I may be wrong, but if I am, no harm's done. If I'm not, I may get a line on the gent who's responsible for all the trouble hereabouts. He's a smooth article with plenty under his hat besides hair, a highly unusual type. A genius gone wrong, and utterly snakeblooded. Killing a man means no more to him than swatting a fly. I think he may actually get a sadistic pleasure from murder. There was no earthly reason for shooting old Hank Givens through the head when he was down on the ground and helpless. That's a sample of his work. In fact, it may be his one weak spot, his yen for violence. I hope so. All set? Put out the light."

Farr did so and removed the bar he had caused to be placed across the back door after the incident of the missing lock bolt. Slade slid through the opening and found himself in the pitch-dark alley, the alley which paralleled the main street and ran past the rear of the Cholla bank. It was well past midnight of a quiet night, with very few people on the streets.

Slade walked swiftly until he had covered better than three blocks and knew he was nearing the bank building, then he slowed his step and took care not to make the slightest sound. He paused often to listen and to peer ahead, his eyes straining to pierce the gloom.

The alley appeared to be deserted. Slade reached the bank building and paused in its rear. Still no sound, no movement. He thought he could discern a faint glow back of one of the windows but could not be sure. Even if there was a light inside the building, it could well be a lamp, turned low, for the convenience of the night watchman who was always on duty. Slade stole on, reached the far corner of the building and almost fell headlong as he tripped over something huddled against the wall. Recovering his balance, he bent over the object, which he explored with his hand.

It was the body of a man, his face sticky with blood that flowed from a deep gash in his forehead. There was little doubt in Slade's mind but that it was what was left of the watchman, who had either left the building on an errand or had been lured out by some suspicious sound, presumably by way of the back door which opened onto the alley near where the body lay. A little light seeped into the alley from the street and Slade could make out its dim rectangle.

He speculated on the door, took a step toward it, then turned and glided around the corner. With cautious steps he made his way to the front of the bank. The massive front door was closed, but through the front windows the faint gleam of light within the building was a little stronger. Slade's keen ears caught a sound, a tiny murmuring that persisted steadily.

Glancing up and down the deserted street, he approached the door, gripped the knob and turned it by almost imperceptible degrees. It turned easily and without sound. Grasping the knob firmly, he pushed slightly. The door moved on its hinges, a thread of crack appeared between it and the jamb. The murmuring sound was louder. He heard the mutter of a voice.

He pushed the door a little more, tensed for a spring. Inside was a prodigious clatter that sounded like a thunderclap in the silence as a chair propped against the door went over. Slade slammed the door wide and bounded inside, slithering along the wall.

A single swift glance showed him a lamp on the floor, its guttering wick turned low. Its lurid glow beat on several men springing erect in front of the door of the ponderous steel vault. A shot rang out, the bullet thudding into the wall.

Both Slade's guns let go, the flashes lighting the weird pandemonium of activity. Back and forth through the smoke gushed the vivid lances of orange flame. Bullets fanned the Ranger's face. One glanced sideways from the wall inches from his head and showered him with splinters. Another ripped the sleeve of his shirt.

Through the uproar knifed a bubbling scream, a death-agony shriek. A body thudded to the floor, metal clanging beside it. A voice bawled an order. Slade caught a fleeting glimpse of wild eyes and a bristling short beard. Then the safe crackers were storming out the back door, Slade's bullets speeding them on their way.

The door banged shut. Slade streaked across the room, slamming one smoking gun into its holster. He seized the knob, turned it. The door resisted his efforts. Fumbling frantically, he found it was secured by a snap lock. By the time he got the bolt released and the door open, horses were pounding up the alley. He emptied his gun after the flickering shadows, but all kept going. In the distance sounded shouts, drawing nearer.

Slade bounded back into the bank and shot a searching glance over the interior. The lamp still burned, guttering and smoking. On the floor lay a hand drill, a crowbar and other tools. There was an almost completed circle of overlapping holes around the combination knob. On the floor lay a man, blood still oozing from the ghastly wound where a slug had torn through his throat. His blood-drenched features were almost unrecognizable as human.

The shouts were drawing nearer. Slade could hear the pound of running feet. He leaped to the back door, flung it open again and raced up the alley at top speed. He was breathing hard when he reached the rear entrance of the Branding Pen. A couple of taps, and the pencil of light seeping under the door vanished. An instant later, the door opened a crack. Slide slipped through. Farr closed the door and dropped the bar into place.

"Light the lamp," Slade said. "Right! Have you got gun cleaning tools handy?"

"In the table drawer," said Farr, speaking for the first time. In silence he watched Slade scoop out rat-tail brushes, rags and oil with one hand, ejecting the spent shells from his guns with the other.

"Shove 'em up the chimney over there, onto the offset," he ordered. Farr hastened to comply. Slade was working on his guns with smooth speed. A few minutes later he reloaded them and slipped them into their holsters.

"Your iron hasn't been fired lately?" he asked Farr. "Okay, shove this stuff up the chimney with the shells. I doubt if he'll think to look there."

"Who?" asked Farr as he did what Slade told him. Slade waved him to the chair on the opposite side of the table, upon which was a bottle and two glasses. He filled the glasses to the brim, leaned back and began rolling a cigarette.

"The sheriff," Slade answered Farr's question. "I'm pretty sure he'll be here mighty soon, asking questions. He'll be almost sure to want to examine my guns; yours too, the chances are. He'll have others with him and I don't want the part I played in the shindig to become generally known, not yet."

Farr blinked in bewilderment. "What the devil happened, can't you tell me?" he pleaded.

"My hunch that they'd make a try for the gold in the bank vault was a straight one," Slade replied. "But I bungled things and all but one got away; he's still in the bank and will stay there till the coroner is ready for him."

He regaled Farr with an account of the unexpected chair against the door and the fight before the bank vault.

"Another ten minutes and they'd have had the knob drilled out and the vault cleaned," he concluded. "A smooth-working bunch. Having already experienced samples of how they overlook nothing, I should have anticipated some sort of a warning device against that door. Guess I was a bit too worked up over the poor devil of watchman to think straight. I'm afraid he's a goner. I didn't have time to examine him closely, but he had suffered a terrible blow on the head, one that should kill a man outright. We'll learn about that shortly, I imagine; he'll be picked up by the bunch hightailing to the bank when they heard the shooting. Expect the sheriff was with them. If not he will be there by now. Take it easy, we're just enjoying a drink in privacy and having a business talk. Unlock the door so they can get in easy; they should be here any minute, now."

Farr did so and they relaxed comfortably in their chairs, sipping their drinks.

"Here they come," Slade chuckled a little later as boots pounded the floor and the jabber in the saloon abruptly stilled. A moment more and the door banged open. Sheriff Cole stood glowering, his head outthrust, hands climped on the butts of his guns. Beside him stood two deputies with cocked rifles.

"Howdy, Sheriff," greeted Slade, apparently oblivious to the menace of rifle and six-gun. "Come in and have a drink on me; sort of chilly out tonight, isn't it?"

As the sheriff gurgled with outraged dignity, Carry Farr arose in wrath.

"What the devil's the idea?" he bellowed. "This is a private room. What do you mean by bustin' in here like you were figuring to stage a holdup?" He glared at the sheriff and his deputies.

The deputies shifted their feet uncomfortably; one surreptitiously lowered the hammer of his rifle.

"Somebody just tried to rob the bank," blurted the sheriff.

"Well, what the devil are you coming here for?" demanded Farr. "This isn't a bank."

With a visible effort the sheriff controlled his temper.

"Listen, Farr," he said quietly, "I'm not aiming to persecute anybody, but I'm an officer of the law, elected by the people of this county and sworn to do my duty. I'm doing it as I see it. That's why I came here tonight. There was shooting in the bank, plenty of it, and there's a dead man lying beside a kit of burglar tools, and blood spots in the alley outside the bank, which seems to indicate that another hellion or two got punctured. Looks like there was a falling out of some sort among the thieves. The night watchman has his head split open—I'm afraid he'll die. Right after the shooting, somebody was heard running up the alley back of your place and seemed to stop here."

"Well?" said Farr.

"I'm not accusing anybody, but this man Slade who's working for you is a new man in the section. There are stories going around about him. I'm not saying they're true or even that they stick close to the real facts, but when things happen like what happened tonight, I can't afford to overlook any bets." He walked steadily across the room, his eyes never leaving Walt Slade; the deputies stiffened and gripped their rifles.

"Feller," the sheriff said, "I'd like to take a look at your guns."

His lips quirking slightly, Slade drew his Colts and laid them on the table. The sheriff picked one up, sniffed at it, glanced at the cylinder, inserted a tentative fingertip in the muzzle. With a grunt he laid the gun down and gave its fellow a similar once-over. Shaking his head and muttering under his mustache, he placed the second gun on the table.

"Okay so far," he rumbled. "Nothing to show they've been shot tonight." His glance traveled over El Halcon from head to foot and again he shook his head. His gaze rested on Slade's table companion.

"Farr," he said, "you're a crippled man and it couldn't have been you running up the alley, but fellers have been known to exchange guns when they don't have time to clean their own. I'd like to take a look at *your* iron."

Carry Farr's lips tightened. He drew his gun and slammed it on the table, cocking it in the same move. The sheriff dodged and swore as the black muzzle spun in his direction. He glared at Farr, picked up the big Colt gingerly and carefully lowered the hammer. A brief examination and he replaced it on the table. His eyes met those of the saloonkeeper squarely.

"I apologize, Farr," he said. "I hope there's no hard feelings."

Once again Walt Slade saw what was undoubtedly a smile in Carry Farr's eyes.

"Forget it, Cole," he said. "No sense in holding an honest mistake against a man who is trying to do the right thing. Have a drink before you go; you, too, deputies."

"Don't mind if I do," said the sheriff. Walt Slade's face wore a very pleased expression as the two clinked glasses.

TWELVE

After the sheriff and his deputies had departed, closing the door behind them, Slade and Farr grinned at each other.

"Well, looks like you and the old gent have buried the hatchet," said the Ranger. "But I'm afraid he still doesn't know what to make of me," he added with a chuckle.

"He's puzzled, all right," agreed Farr.

"Glad the watchman wasn't cashed in," Slade remarked. "Chances are he'll recover. A blow like that usually either kills a man outright or doesn't do him lasting damage. Barring a bad skull fracture and resulting brain injury, Doc Cooper should be able to pull him through. Doc is mighty good at such things; I'm glad he decided to move his office down here. Harding is quite peaceful but in Cholla he'll get rich."

"Especially if El Halcon sticks around to keep the pot boiling," Farr chuckled. "You've known Doc a long time?"

"Quite a few years and in various places," Slade replied. "He's a typical frontier doctor; got itchy feet and can't keep still in one place for over long. He's helped me quite a bit every now and then. Nothing much he misses and the information a doctor is able to give a peace officer is often very valuable."

A tap sounded on the door leading to the saloon. Farr opened it to reveal Howard Hunter.

"Why, hello," said Farr. "Come in, Hunter, what's on your mind?"

Hunter nodded and sauntered in; Farr closed the door behind him.

There was a mocking expression on Hunter's handsome face as he paused at the table and looked Walt Slade squarely in the eyes. Slade's own eyes scanned Hunter's countenance an instant with a keen and searching glance which dropped to the index finger of Hunter's left hand and held there a moment before rising to meet Hunter's glittering gaze.

Smiling sardonically, Hunter laid an exploded .45 cartridge on the table. He stood it on end and tapped it lightly with a tapering, sensitive finger.

"I picked up this shell, and a couple more like it, in the bank when I got there just as the sheriff was getting ready to leave," he observed in pleasantly conversational tones. "Noticed something funny about it. The firing pin of the gun that shot it hits the cap quite a long ways off center. That firing pin would sort of stand out in any company. Fact is, if I was the man who owned that gun I'd be traveling away from this section without delay, and traveling fast."

His snapping blue eyes never left Slade's face. El Halcon sat rigid, staring at him, lips slightly parted.

"Yes, I'd sure be traveling—if I happened to be that man," Hunter repeated. With a pleasant nod he turned and sauntered out of the room, leaving Slade and Farr gazing at each other. After a long moment the latter spoke.

"Who'd have figured that slick-faced hellion to be that smart?" he demanded. "Picking up those shells and noticing the off-center marking on the caps! He has no use for me and this is his way of taking a slap at me. He'll show those other shells he's got to the sheriff and Cole will come charging back here asking more questions, and asking to see the firing pins of your guns, which'll mean trouble for you. Say! What's so darn funny? I don't see anything to laugh about."

"You and Hunter have one thing in common, you jump at conclusions a bit too hastily," Slade smiled. "Get those shells from the chimney, the ones you watched me eject from my guns."

Farr fumbled the exploded cartridges from where he had perched them on the offset and came back wiping the soot from his fingers. Slade stood them on end, all twelve of them.

"Take a look at the cap markings," he said. Farr did so, and swore. The firing pin dents on the caps were perfectly centered.

"Yes, Hunter was a mite hasty in jumping at conclusions," Slade repeated. "As it happened, I didn't eject any spent shells in the bank—I didn't have time—but it looks like one of the safe crackers did, and Hunter picked them up. I figured it was a good idea to let him fool himself for a while, and he won't go to the sheriff, even when he realizes he didn't scare me out of town. In fact, I'm glad this happened, for it tells me how much Hunter knows and what he doesn't know, which is all to the good."

"Well, I'll be hanged!" sputtered Farr. "That smart hellion is too smart for his own good; he'll burn his fingers yet."

"I noticed he has a bad burn on one tonight," remarked Slade. "As if he'd touched a hot poker with it. By the way, does Hunter ever wear glasses, do you happen to know?"

"Heck, no!" grunted Farr. "That jigger's got shootin' eyes; he can knock off a gnat's wing at twenty paces. Why?"

"If you had looked close, you would have noticed little indentures in the flesh just to the front of his ears, the sort of traces tight fitting glasses will leave," Slade replied. "Hunter made a bad mistake by coming here tonight, so soon after the attempted bank robbery."

"How's that?" asked Farr.

"The burn on his finger," Slade said slowly, "is the kind of burn that would be made by the overheated steel bit of a high-power drill going at top speed, should the manipulator of the drill happen to touch it in a moment of excitement. And the indentures in the flesh to the front of his ears could be made by the spring-steel clamps that hold a false beard in place."

Farr stared, his mouth dropping open. "You don't mean—" he began incredulously.

"Yes, that's exactly what I mean," Slade interrupted. "Howard Hunter is the head of the Cholla Raiders and guilty of the murders of half a dozen men, probably more. He is also guilty of stealing highgrade ore from the Comstock mine and crushing it in his own mill, although how he does it I'm hanged if I know, and until I do know, I have no case against him that would stand up in court. A smart lawyer would get him off scot-free, and make me look like a fool, if I tried to press a charge on the very circumstantial evidence I now have."

"How do you know he is stealing the high-grade?" asked the bewildered saloonkeeper.

"Remember the other day we watched the gold ingots from Hunter's mill being carried into the bank and I asked you if Hunter owned more than one mine?" Farr nodded.

"There are two kinds of gold," Slade resumed. "One is yellow gold, the other is red gold. The difference in colorization is often very slight, but can be noted by one with keen eyes, a knowledge of geological peculiarities and some experience in mining. I got a good look at those ingots and realized that the gold they represented could not possibly have come from the same mine—the ledges would be entirely different. Some of the ingots had a distinct reddish tinge. The next day I got a look at the ingots from the Comstock mill; they were all red gold."

"Well, I'll be hanged!" sputtered Farr.

"I think Hunter, undoubtedly an experienced mining man with an exhaustive knowledge of quartz mining, was shrewd enough to mix the stolen ore with the product of his own mine before crushing it, but he slipped a little on one batch," Slade added. "The color showed."

"Wonder why John Mosby didn't catch on to the difference in the gold?" asked Farr.

"Mosby is not a mining man in the real sense of the word," Slade replied. "All his experience was with placer mining—panning shallow streams, digging out pockets of nuggets that in the course of ages had been washed down from some parent ledge. By his own admission, he knew nothing of quartz mining until Hunter came along. He could recognize a gold-bearing ledge when he hit upon one—witness the Comstock—but that's about as far as his knowledge goes. Besides, he had not the slightest reason to suspect Hunter of any wrongdoing, nor had anybody else. Hunter is smart, far above the average in intelligence, but the owlhoot brand always make little slips, like the one he made by coming here tonight and confirming what I already believed."

"The snake-blooded varmint!" exploded Farr.

"Yes, he's all of that," Slade said wearily. "Absolutely without conscience or mercy. And if I don't manage to stop him soon, very likely some more innocent people will die."

"And he figures you, as El Halcon, are here to horn in on his good thing?"

"So I presume," Slade acceded.

"And meanwhile, unless you watch your step mighty, mighty close, your life ain't worth a busted cartridge," growled Farr. "You'd be a lot safer if he knew you are a Ranger."

"And then he'd cover up in a hurry and I'd never get a line on him," Slade answered. "I wouldn't be surprised if he's already planning to close up shop soon; he must have plenty stashed away. He'll pay off his bunch and they'll scatter."

"Some of 'em might try to blackmail him," observed Farr.

"And all it would get them would be a grave," Slade replied. "Their sort are never long on brains, but they have enough to realize that. And besides, they could never get away with it. The word of one of their kind against that of a reputable citizen and respected business man? The very people he has victimized would be the first to rally to his defense. No, I have to get him dead to rights in a loop he can't slip out of. And the chances are when and if the showdown comes, he'll go out fighting. He'd prefer hot lead to a rope."

"He'll get one or the other," Farr declared

confidentially. "What's your next move, if you don't mind telling me?"

"Tomorrow I'm riding to Harding to do a little telegraphing," Slade replied.

"You don't figure the Raiders will make a try for the gold shipment going to Harding tomorrow?"

"Not with a couple of guards and half a dozen outriders convoying the shipment," Slade smiled. "That's why Hunter made a try for the bank. He knows he couldn't buck that kind of opposition and is too smart to try."

"By the way," remarked Farr, "your *amigo* Park Crony is in circulation again. He's been keeping under cover since you busted his gunhand for him, but I guess it's in shape to use again."

"Crony might be a chink in Hunter's armor," Slade observed thoughtfully. "Shrewd enough in some ways, but with a penchant for doing stupid things when he has a few snorts under his belt."

"He's bad," grunted Farr.

"Yes," Slade agreed, "but not smart enough to be really dangerous. Well, I'll look over things in the other room."

Slade did ride to Harding the following day. On the way he passed the stage and its convoy bearing the gold shipment to the railroad town. Sheriff Cole, who also accompanied the shipment, looked slightly startled as El Halcon circled the convoy, but he displayed no rancor and answered Slade's greeting with a wave of his hand.

"I sure can't make that big jigger out," he complained to one of the guards. "Despite the yarns going around about him, he seems okay."

"Well," replied the guard, "speaking for myself, I'd sure rather have him for me than against me."

"I've a notion you've got something there," acceded the sheriff.

Arriving at Harding, Slade at once repaired to the railroad telegraph office, where he dictated a long message that caused the operator to regard him with lively interest. The message was addressed to the branch assay office at Carson City, where the gold from the Comstock mines was shipped for purchase.

"There should be an answer within a couple of hours or so," he told the operator. "Hold it for me."

As he spoke he slipped something from a cunningly concealed secret pocket in his broad leather belt and held it before the eyes of the operator. It was the famous silver star set on a silver circle, the feared and honored badge of the Texas Rangers.

"The rules of your company forbid you to reveal to anyone the contents of any message sent over the wires," he said. "I am personally requesting that in this instance the rule be strictly observed."

"Don't worry, sir, it'll be observed," the operator declared with emphasis.

Later, Slade received the reply from the assay

office, which he read with satisfaction. He spent the night in Harding, heading back to Cholla at dawn. Riding at a leisurely pace, he reached the mining town sometime after dark.

"It ties up," he told Carry Farr. "The assay office reports two types of gold in Hunter's shipment. Of course they can't say that the red gold came from the Comstock, but they do say the two specimens show a marked similarity, which corroborates my suspicion."

"So now all you have to do is drop a loop on the hellion, eh?" said Farr.

"Yes," Slade replied dryly, "that's all."

THIRTEEN

The following night, Slade showed up for work at the usual time. Shortly afterward, however, he and Carry Farr repaired to the back room and closed and locked the door.

"Everything's under control," said Farr. "You've got the boys so tamed nobody will start anything, and the dealers and wheel men are so honest they can't recognize their faces in a mirror. Nobody will know you're not around and I can take care of things without trouble. What you want to do is take care of yourself; you're up against a salty bunch and a smart one."

"I think practically all the brains belong to the head of the outfit," Slade replied. "He's a slippery customer, all right, though, and hard to figure. Maybe I'll get a break. Hope so; I need one."

With a nod, Farr extinguished the lamp and opened the rear door that led to the alley. Slade slipped out and reached the stable by a round-about way through deserted side streets. He swiftly got the rig on Shadow and ten minutes later found him riding cautiously into the gloomy mouth of Dry Water Canyon.

The night was very dark, but the sky was brilliant with stars that cast a faint glow which was bright enough to outline objects. The mountains were in blue-black silhouette against the silvered sky, with a dappling of clouds in the west. The shadows were black under the ghost-like sentinel trees that stood guard over the lesser growth. The silence was so intense as to be felt as a tangible thing pressing down on the lone horseman. The scene was one of utter loneliness, but with a crisp edge of expectancy hard to define.

Across the canyon from the site of the Comstock mine, Slade pulled to a halt in the gloom of the growth which flanked the cliffs. For a long while he studied the site of the mine, wondering if it were possible to tap its shafts and corridors by means of a short tunnel. Finally he shook his head. He had learned that the rich pockets of ore were almost wholly confined to the lower galleries a good five hundred feet beneath the earth's surface. It just wasn't possible to reach them by any known means of excavation that could be kept secret. He rode on, slowly, scanning the cliffs, the canyon floor, which soon discovered its downward slope. After a while he reached the stretch of soft earth which had shown the puzzling prints of horses and mules.

"Somewhere along here, horse, is the answer," he told Shadow, "but where it is and what it is is beyond me. What do you think?"

Shadow gave a snort that might have meant anything, or nothing. Slade chuckled, hooked a long leg over the saddle horn and rolled a cigarette. After finishing his smoke he rode back up the canyon for a mile or so, where he had noted a low mound of earth and rock at the edge of the brush, from which eminence he would have a good view in every direction while he himself remained in the shadow. Here he took up his post.

As does the fierce, fearless, unerring bird for which he was named sit on crag or topmost bough waiting for its kill, he sat his tall black horse, every sense at a vigilant alert. Until the golden stars turned to silver, the sunlight glanced off the leaves and the grasses burned purple and amethyst with a gemming of dew. Then with a disgusted glance around, he left his perch and rode swiftly up the gorge, skirting the Comstock mine and reaching the canyon mouth before the ore wagons began rumbling over the ruts.

Night after night he kept his lonely vigil, until he grew heartily tired of the business. After a night of lashing rain and wailing wind, he was tempted to give up the whole affair; looked like his hunch wasn't a straight one, after all.

But the next night was a night of brilliant moonlight with only a gentle breeze faintly rustling the leaves, and welling out of the east he heard the tell-tale drumming of fast hoofs. Tense, alert, he watched a troop of horsemen—he counted nine altogether—sweep past. He noted that one of the two big men riding in front kept his right hand thrust into his shirt front. Very likely Park Crony, still solicitous of the injured member. Seen in the moonlight, lost in the shadow, seen in the moonlight again, the ghostly riders drifted down the sinister canyon until the gloom had swallowed them up.

Slade followed, as close as he dared, which wasn't very close, for the moon flame funneling into the gorge made the scene almost as bright as day. However, he knew well they could not turn aside. On either hand the perpendicular rock walls crowded close; a goat could not scale them, much less a troop of horsemen. He was alert, however, against a possible ambush or prematurely running into the mysterious horsemen.

Into the lowering depths of the gorge he pursued his way, peering, listening. He reached the beginning of the half-mile stretch of naked rock. Here he slowed Shadow's pace, for the gorge bent in a shallow curve which greatly lessened the range of his vision. Finally he had the big black progressing at a slow walk. With the greatest caution he rounded a final bulge and directly ahead lay the expanse of stiff clay, its surface almost fluid from the rain of the night before. With an incredulous exclamation he pulled up. Nowhere on the placid expanse, into which a horse's hoof would sink to the fetlock, was a fresh print leading down the canyon. None leading up it, either, for that matter. The troop of night riders had vanished as if they had never been.

Slade swore in exasperation; once again the quarry had eluded him in some mysterious fashion. He glared at the rock walls, the narrow stretches of dense and thorny bush, and found no answer to his unspoken question—where in the devil did they go? The hellions were neither flies nor lizards, although they might be pretty closely related to both pests. Shadow snorted cheerful agreement.

"I tell you they just naturally *couldn't* have gone up the side walls anywhere, and that belt of brush isn't wide enough to hide them," he insisted to the horse.

Shadow snorted again and rolled a derisive eye. "Well, where in blazes did they go then?" he seemed to ask.

"We'll find out," Slade told him grimly, "if I have to ride your legs down to your knees to do it! They had to go somewhere."

But the indubitable fact remained that somewhere along that stretch of rocky floor he had lost the quarry. Tediously, painstakingly, he began zigzagging back up the canyon through the clear moonlight, meticulously examining every foot of the towering side walls, peering into every thicket that appeared denser or wider than the average, riding around outcroppings of rock to view all sides. And discovered nothing. He was so exasperated that he threw caution to the winds and would have been easy prey to any lurking drygulcher; which was evidence of his state of mind and quite unlike the usually canny El Halcon. Finally, locating a spot where he would be fairly safe from the peering eyes of anybody riding the canyon, he holed up and waited.

The dawn came, flaming in the east. The sun arose in glory and with a flashing of ten thousand spears, and it was day. And still the gorge lay silent and deserted save for the choir of little feathered songsters who seemed to mock him with their warbling. At last, in utter disgust, he gave up and rode home to bed.

That night Slade appeared for work at the Branding Pen at the usual hour.

"No luck," he answered Carry Farr's questioning glance. "I saw them, and I'm pretty sure one of the pair riding in front was Park Crony, but somewhere in that darn snake hole I lost them. They just seemed to evaporate in thin air. Did you learn anything?"

"I had the Cattlemen's Club watched, as you asked me to," Farr replied. "Hunter was not there last night, nor all day today. Do you think that means anything?"

"Might mean plenty," Slade said. "Sort of ties up with my belief that he was one of the bunch I saw skalley-hooting down the canyon. His place still watched?"

"Pete is there now," answered Farr. "Not much that Pete misses, and he can pretend to be drunk when he's cold sober in a way that'll fool even a barkeep. Maybe we'll hear something from him later."

"I hope so," Slade said. "The way those side-winders are in sight one minute and aren't the next is enough to aggravate a saint."

"It's hole-in-the-wall country, and that sort of snakes know where to creep," Farr observed in comforting tones.

Slade's gaze fixed for a moment on the saloon-keeper's face; the concentration furrow between his black brows deepened.

"Hole-in-the-wall country," he repeated. "Hole in the wall."

"Yep, it's all of that," Farr nodded. They left the back room and entered the saloon.

Slade was thoughtful as he ate his midnight meal. Once he repeated again Farr's remark, "Hole-in-the-wall country. Hole in the wall! That could be the answer, but in the name of blazes, how and where?"

Pete, to whom the chore of keeping tabs on the Cattlemen's Club had been given, appeared a little later. He sauntered over to where Carry Farr stood at the end of the bar and engaged him in low-voiced conversation. While Pete was having a drink, Farr moved to Slade's table and sat down.

"Hunter's at the Cattlemen's Club right now," he told El Halcon. "Got in just a little while ago. Peter said he looked like he'd been riding."

"I'm pretty sure he had been," Slade replied grimly, "but I still don't know where he spent the past twenty-four hours."

"No reports of robbings or killings come in of late," remarked Farr. "Looks like wherever he was, he wasn't very active."

"May have been a lot more active than we think," Slade differed. "I don't think he was off somewhere picking blackberries. Well, if I can learn where he spent those hours, the whole business may clear up. And I'm sure going to try and find out. I'm knocking off an hour early; I want to look at that canyon by midnight."

"Go to it," said Farr. "Better luck this time. Is there anything I can do to help? I'm a pretty good shot and I can ride."

"Wouldn't be surprised if I need you, later," Slade replied. "How you and the sheriff making out?"

"We had quite a gabfest this afternoon," Farr replied, and shook with silent laughter. "This one will make you grin," he chortled. "Old Wes had been sucking coffee through his mustache and saying nothing. Then all of a sudden he said, 'You know, Carry, I've been thinking about that young feller Slade. He shouldn't be gallivanting around the country like he is, shooting folks without proper law backing. I'm going to have a talk with the Commissioners and I'm pretty sure they'll go along with me. I'm going to give him a job as a deputy sheriff—I can use another good man. Then he can put his gun-slinging talents to a proper use and be so busy he won't have time to get in trouble. Don't you think that's a prime notion?"

Farr paused to drink some coffee himself. "I could hardly keep my face straight, but I told him I thought it was," he concluded. "What do *you* think of *that?*"

Slade smiled, and his cold eyes were abruptly all kindness. "I think it is about as nice a compliment as I've received for some time," he replied.

FOURTEEN

Once more the dark hour before the dawn found Slade riding swiftly down Dry Water Canyon. This time he did not draw rein when he reached the soft ground below the stretch of rocky soil but continued for some little distance in the strengthening light, slowing Shadow to a walk. Finally he found what he was looking for, a dense thicket in which was a small pool of rainwater and a scanty growth of grass.

"Okay, feller," he told the big black. "This should hold you till I get back, so just take it easy for a while."

Shadow offered no objection, so, after flipping the bit from his mouth and loosening the cinches. Slade left him to his own devices, knowing that the intelligent and obedient animal would not stray from the thicket. Then he headed back up the canyon on foot, keeping close to the belt of growth which fringed the western cliffs, where the light was strongest.

With the most painstaking care he examined every foot of the ground, the cliffs, and the growth. He crossed the patch of soft earth and became even more meticulous in his examination, for he was convinced that somewhere along the stretch of almost bare rock was that for which he sought. Somewhere along the mile or so of the outcropping was the way to the hideout of the Cholla Raiders.

But as he toiled along in the ever increasing heat, the quest grew more and more discouraging. Nowhere showed anything that remotely resembled a way up the cliffs, or a wider belt of chaparral. The growth remained unbroken, no signs of passage, and it would have been impossible for horses to force their way through the tangle without leaving evidence of their passing. His progress was very slow and it was well past noon when he reached the north terminus of the strip. Gloomy and disgusted, he sat down on a boulder and rolled a cigarette which proved tasteless in the blistering heat.

Pinching out the butt, he rose to his feet and walked across the canyon to the east wall and renewed his search, with no better success. He was but a few hundred yards from the beginning of the clayey soil, with the shadows already growing long, when he noticed something that quickened his interest.

It wasn't much, just a slight difference in coloration. At the point where he paused, instead of the prevailing dusty looking green, the growth for several yards was slightly yellowish-brown in appearance and the leaves were a trifle withered. His keen eyes probed the patch and he whistled softly under his breath.

"The brush has been cut away here, sure as blazes!" he muttered. "Cut away and then set back in place. Why the dickens couldn't I have thought of that before! An old trick, but a good one if handled properly. Almost certain to fool a man on horseback. One on foot, for that matter, if the devils hadn't gotten a bit careless and failed to replace the fading growth with fresh bushes. This looks like a real lead."

Slade knew better than to remove the cut growth which had been so cleverly put back in place while it was still green and none of the foliage jarred loose. Now any attempt to tug the cut ends of the trunks from the earth would result in a shower of dead leaves which would show keen eyes that the subterfuge had been discovered and investigated by somebody. Which the Ranger did not wish to happen. He moved down the canyon a few yards and with utmost care wormed his way through the dense and thorny chaparral. As he expected, the growth thinned somewhat as he drew near the rock wall and he was able, by hugging the face of the cliff, to inch along silently. He was not surprised when he wriggled through a final fringe and found himself in a narrow lane cut through the brush, a lane that ended where an opening split the face of the cliff, an opening wide enough to admit two horses abreast, and perhaps eight feet in height. And the lane showed evidence that horses had passed that way no great time before.

However, there were no signs of their presence at the moment. The cave mouth, for such it undoubtedly was, yawned dark and silent. Slade glided to the lip of the opening and paused uncertain; and like an unexpected nightmare vision, a man suddenly arose from behind a boulder within arm's reach.

Slade caught the flash of metal, weaved sideways and clutched the lunging knife hand with fingers like rods of nickel steel. A fist crashed against his jaw and he went down, still clinging to the corded wrist, taking the attacker with him.

Over and over they rolled amid the rocks, grimly silent, striking, wrenching, fighting with life as the stake. Slade held the fellow's knife hand helpless and lashed out with his other fist.

But the man, lean and rangy, was quick as he was strong. He dodged the blow and, with the Ranger slightly off balance, tore his knife hand free and surged back and erect. Slade hurled himself face down in a split second of time. Over his prostrate body the thrown knife buzzed like an angry hornet.

Slade whipped to his knees, hands flashing down. He saw the black muzzle of a gun yawning toward him as his own Colts roared deafeningly.

A bullet screeched past the Ranger's ear as the man, dead on his feet, pulled the trigger with a last convulsive spasm of his muscles. Slade leaped to his feet as he fell, guns jutting forward. Then he holstered the Colts and for a long moment stood listening.

But after the echoes of the triple report had ceased to slam among the rocks, the silence remained unbroken. Taking no chances, Slade slipped into the brush and waited a while longer. Nothing happened. The cave mouth gave no evidence of life, nor did the narrow lane through the brush. Reassured by the continued lack of sound, he ejected the spent shells from his guns and replaced them with fresh cartridges. Another moment of listening and he stepped to the body and turned it over to. show a dark, distorted face and black eyes already fixed in death. The dead man's pockets showed nothing of significance other than a large sum of money, which Slade replaced. Then he rocked back on his heels, rolled a cigarette and reviewed the situation.

The dead man had evidently been set to guard the cave mouth against any possible intruder, another example of Howard Hunter's thoroughness and meticulous care of all details. Which, Slade decided, tended to indicate that there was nobody inside the cave. He resolved to risk exploring it.

First, however, he dragged the body some distance from the cut in the brush, jammed it into a narrow crevice and covered it with loose stones. Next he carefully removed everything that hinted at conflict, replacing overturned boulders, straightening bent branches, covering the blood spots with a sifting of loose earth. Satisfied that all was as it was before, he again approached the cave mouth.

Slade found himself in a quandary. Should he go groping along in the dark, he might tumble into some awful hole or get lost in a maze of side tunnels that were often incidental to such burrows. On the other hand, if he carried a light he would advertise his presence to anyone who might be lurking in the gloomy corridor. After due reflection he decided that to wander about in the dark was the greater risk.

Sotol grew among the chaparral near the cliff base. Slade broke off several dry stalks which would afford excellent torches. Lighting one, he set out on his perilous exploration. The sotol burned slowly with a clear flame which disclosed walls and a ceiling of dark rock. The rock floor was fairly smooth. Very quickly Slade was convinced that a large body of water had once flowed down the tunnel to reach the outer air. The mystery of the river which was no longer in evidence was explained.

The cave curved shortly beyond its mouth to pursue a uniformly northeastern direction. The air was fresh and a slight draft soughed down the tunnel, which Slade was at a loss to explain. It was hardly strong enough to denote a nearby second opening, and it was damp. He shook his head and continued, keeping close to the east wall, pausing often to peer and listen.

Abruptly he heard a sound from no great distance ahead, the ringing click of a shod hoof stamping the rock floor. Instantly he extinguished his torch and stood listening.

The sound was repeated, but no nearer; it appeared to be stationary. After a long and breathless wait, the Ranger crept on through the dark, hugging the rock wall, testing the ground with each forward step before resting his weight on it. A third time he heard the stamp of a hoof, nearer now and apparently a little to the right. A dozen more cautious steps and he could hear the breathing of animals, then an impatient snort. Without doubt horses or other quadrupeds were tethered somewhere in the darkness ahead, but so far he had heard nothing that indicated human occupancy of the tunnel.

Once again he stood motionless, listening. Abruptly he arrived at a decision and relighted the torch. The flame burned up and revealed that the cave had widened to a large room with rock walls. Here the roof was so high above his head as to be invisible in the torch light. The torn and jagged walls suggested that the room had been hollowed out by some tremendous explosion of steam or gas rather than by the action of water.

Over to one side, with feed boxes under their noses and water handy, were a half dozen mules and a single horse. They pricked inquiring ears and gazed mildly at the Ranger with an air of expectancy. Evidently they were accustomed to human visitors and showed no surprise at his sudden appearance.

What interested Slade more were neatly stacked stout canvas sacks filled to bulging with something. And nearby was a heap of rawhide "packsaddles," which the cowboy calls "kyacks" or "aperejos," and which, when filled, fit snugly over a mule's back and under its belly.

With quick lithe steps, Slade crossed to where the filled sacks were stacked. A quick inspection showed that their contents was ore, doubtless highgrade, which it was logical to believe came from John Mosby's Comstock mine.

Here was the "clearing house" of the Cholla Raiders. Here the ore purloined from the Comstock was stored to await transportation, via mule back, to Howard Hunter's stamp mill. How did they get the ore from the mine? That question was still to be resolved, and Slade was determined to find the answer.

The big cave provided plenty of evidence of extensive occupancy. Against one wall a rough stone fireplace had been constructed, the stones blackened by many fires. Shelves supported by pegs driven in crevices in the walls were heaped with staple provisions. Cooking utensils hung from other pegs. There were several rude bunks on which lay tumbled blankets. Pails contained water that was sweet and fresh to the taste. All in all, it was a very sumptuous hangout for a gang of desperadoes.

In the wall opposite the opening by way of which Slade had entered was another and somewhat larger opening, apparently a continuation of the tunnel which led to the outer air.

Slade studied the opening a moment, then his gaze went back to the horse that without doubt belonged to the dead outlaw he had stuffed in the crevice. A plan was forming in his mind, and the presence of the animal in the cave would be a flaw that would very likely wreck the plan. When the rest of the bunch put in an appearance, which Slade reasoned they would do in the near future, and found the horse with its owner missing, they would naturally become suspicious and be on guard. But were man and horse both missing they would be more apt to think little of it, surmising that the fellow had abandoned his post and ridden off for some purpose of his own. At least he hoped that would be their reaction, and he believed it would be.

Hanging on a peg were a saddle and bridle, the only rig in evidence. Slade quickly cinched the saddle in place, adjusted the bridle and mounted. He snuffed out the torch that still burned fitfully, being careful to retain the charred butt to discard outside the cave, mounted and sent the horse down the tunnel to the open air. There were no pitfalls or obstructions, he knew, so he rode at a good pace.

When he reached the outside, he dismounted and sidled the horse down-canyon along the cliff face until he reached a spot where the growth was a trifle thinner than average. He swung into the saddle again and at the expense of a few scratches and some lost skin for himself and his mount forced his way through the tangle. He continued until he was well along on the expanse of soft earth. Removing the rig he hid it in a thicket and turned the horse loose to fend for itself. The animal would not return up canyon to the barren terrain, but would wander on south to where there was grass and a little water. Night was not far off, and even were it seen by somebody headed for the cave it was highly unlikely that it would be recognized in the gloom.

With this detail cared for, Slade made his way back through the deepening dusk to the cave. He lighted a torch and without mishap reached the rock-walled room that he was convinced was the hole-up of the Cholla Raiders.

After a final glance around, he crossed the big cave and entered the far opening, questing forward with his torch. He had progressed for perhaps half a mile when he became conscious of a low murmuring somewhere ahead, which loudened as he continued and resolved into the sound of a body of running water.

Louder and louder grew the sound until the light of the torch revealed the curving lip of a broad and deep stream that emerged from an opening in the side wall and plunged into a gulf upon the edge of which he stood.

As he gazed into the black depths, Slade's scalp prickled. Up from the darkness came but the faintest of liquid whisperings. The depth of the chasm was tremendous.

"Blazes! What a hole!" he exclaimed. "The water that once ran down the canyon!" Quite likely the convulsion untold years before which hollowed out the cave he had just quitted had at the same time opened the chasm and diverted the stream into it.

The near side of the gulf was not sheer, at first. It sloped downward steeply, studded with shallow ledges and fangs of rock, before, about twenty feet below, it plummeted into nothingness.

For long moments Slade stood staring fascinated at that curving lip of water which smoked over the edge of the gulf less than a dozen yards from where he stood. That endlessly overturning dome had a hypnotic effect. With a startled oath, he realized that he was unconsciously leaning toward the opening at his feet. He tore his eyes from the oily, down-rushing curve, cautiously skirted the chasm, there being room to walk between its edge and the side wall of the cave, and continued on his way.

There was plenty of evidence that he was not the first to tread the sinister path. His boots crunched on bits of fallen ore and he saw cigarette butts and other things that denoted men had been using the tunnel over a considerable period of time.

He had proceeded slowly for several hundred yards through the gloomy burrow when abruptly he halted with an exclamation. Before him was a flight of rude but solidly built steps leading upward to an opening that pierced the wall of the tunnel. His pulses quickening with excitement, and with increased caution, he crept up the steps to find himself in a shallow side tunnel that had undoubtedly been cut in the rock, which here was shattered and crumbling, by the hand of man. And only a few yards distant was a wooden door. He approached the barrier warily, paused and listened for several minutes. Then he gingerly tried the door, which opened outward from where he stood.

Delicately balanced on oiled hinges, the barrier swung easily to the pressure of his hand and he found himself in another tunnel dark as the one he had just left.

But this was no natural passage blown out by exploding gases of volcanic origin; this was a man-made gallery in the depths of the mountain. The roof was supported by heavy timbers, as were also the side walls at regular intervals. The floor was smooth and level. A glance showed him that the door through which he had come was cunningly designed to appear but a part of the supporting timbering of the bore.

It was without doubt the worked-out gallery of a mine, and it took no great stretch of the imagination to resolve it as a drift of the Comstock lower levels. The levels that at the north end of Dry Water Canyon were a good five hundred feet below the earth's surface, but here, due to the downward slope of the gorge, were about on a level with the canyon floor. The man who had conceived and executed the method of tapping the Comstock's highgrade ledges was an engineer and a good one.

His curiosity at a high pitch, Slade moved along the old tunnel. On the floor were tell-tale bits of ore and at one point he saw a burst sack, its contents spilled, lying beside one of the supporting timbers.

And then, to confirm his deductions, there came to his ears a muffled booming sound from somewhere ahead. It was a distant dynamite explosion. A little later another sound threaded through the darkness, thin with distance, that he recognized as the purring chatter of steam or air driven drills.

His next-to-last torch was flickering out, casting but a faint and lurid glow against the encroaching wall of the darkness. Just one more stalk left; he didn't want that one to burn out before he passed the deadly chasm in the cave floor. Time to be retracing his steps.

And then he saw, some distance ahead, a number of winking lights drifting toward him. Somebody, several somebodies, were coming down the gallery. Quickly extinguishing the last sparks of the torch, he turned and hurried back the way he had come through the utter darkness. He was not particularly perturbed, for it was highly unlikely that the dying flicker of his torch had been seen, and whoever were headed down the tunnel were proceeding at a leisurely pace. He would have no difficulty reaching the outer air ahead of them, if they continued that far.

With the plainsman's sense of distance, he knew when he was nearing the wooden door and slowed his pace. A moment later and his outstretched hand touched it. He swung it open, closing it softly behind him, and glided down the steps to the floor of the natural cave. Hugging the rock wall, he hurried along until he heard the murmur of the stream rushing into the chasm and felt the dank breath of the gulf on his face. He slowed down, edging ahead carefully. Directly opposite the seemingly bottomless hole he halted and stood rigid.

Once again he saw lights, six or seven of them, bobbing along and steadily drawing nearer. A second group was heading *up* the cave, very likely to join with the men coming down the old mine tunnel. *He was trapped!*

FIFTEEN

Standing rigid in the darkness, Slade's brain worked at lightning speed, forming plans, quickly discarding them. Behind him was death. Coming steadily toward him from the front was death. By his side was death in the frightful chasm plunging down to earth's heart.

He glanced toward the approaching lights; they were steadily drawing nearer. Now he could hear the voices of those who carried them; he had little more than seconds in which to chart a plan of action. A wild notion of charging the bunch and shooting his way through fleeted through his mind, but was quickly discarded. There were six or seven men in the group. The odds were too heavy against him. Such a course would be tantamount to committing suicide. He concentrated on the situation with an earnestness that almost amounted to mental agony, and could see no way out of the dilemma. His face was wet with sweat and the slight draft soughing up from the chasm beat pleasantly on his heated flesh.

An inspiration flashed through his brain. The chasm! Its rock-studded near side which sloped down to the offset some twenty feet below before it took the final dizzy plunge! Perhaps he could slip over the lip, slide down the slope and find a resting place before hurtling over the offset. An appalling choice, but it appeared he had no other. To remain where he was meant certain death. Better to take the terrible risk on the chance it might be successful.

The thought was parent to the deed. He eased his body over the edge, feet first, and began inching his way down the slope. It was frightfully steep and the hand holds were few and far between. But if he could just get down a dozen feet or so without disaster, he might be able to hang there until the approaching outlaws had passed. Then he would try to scramble up again and reach the outside before they returned.

Another unexpected and terrifying complication arose. Just as his face cleared the chasm edge he saw, coming from the direction of the mine corridor, another cluster of lights.

Too late to do anything about it, even were there anything to do. He concentrated on groping his way down the slope. Once he was forced to slide a little distance, not knowing if he would ever come to rest again. With a thrill of horror he felt one foot encounter nothing but empty space; he had reached the offset!

His clutching hand gripped a knob of stone and in the nick of time stayed his progress into the depths. He hung on with the strength of despair, enduring the terrific strain, afraid to grope about for a second handhold, for now the group coming up the cave was almost to the chasm. They were talking loudly in carefree tones, evidently suspecting nothing untoward.

A shout sounded from the direction of the mine. It was answered in kind by those coming up the cave. On the lip of the gulf the two groups merged. Slade knew that did one chance to hold out his lantern and glance down he was almost certain to be detected.

"A load waiting for you by the door, and more coming," a voice said. "We'll pack this load to the big cave and come back to give you a hand with the rest."

"Okay," said another voice. "Did you see anything of Hank? He wasn't around when we came in."

"Haven't seen him," replied the first voice. "Reckon he slipped off somewhere for a drink or something; he's good at that."

"He'd better have a darned good excuse for not being at his post," the other voice countered grimly, "or the boss will slip him something he won't like."

Slade found a crumb of comfort in the situation. Appeared the suspicions of the outlaws had not been aroused by the absence of the guard. Then all his energies concentrated again on his own predicament.

For the two groups had separated, one heading down the cave, the other continuing toward the mine. He was still trapped. The fingers of his hand were growing numb with strain, and both feet were hanging over the offset. Taking a chance of being heard, he groped about frantically with his free hand. With a surge of relief he encountered another fang of stone. He gripped it, made sure it was secure, and let go with his other hand, rejoicing in the relief afforded his aching muscles. He flexed the stiff fingers until they were something like normal. Grasping the knobs with both hands, he slowly drew himself up a bit. One foot found a purchase on a tiny ledge and eased the strain on his arms somewhat. A terrible fear was numbing his mind. What if he should be unable to climb back up the slope! The probability was too vivid to be disregarded. For a moment he experienced a surge of sheer panic. With a mighty effort of the will he recovered his self-control and concentrated on retaining his perilous balance on the steep slope. The hiss and murmur of the falling water dinned mockingly in his ears. It seemed to chortle at his predicament. "Just wait!" said the sibilant whisper. *Just wait! Your strength is going. Soon your fingers will grow stiff and numb. Then your hold will loosen and the unplumbed depths will claim their prey. Just wait!*

Slade ground his teeth together and tried to shut his ears to the derisive mutter.

Once again he heard footsteps approaching. And once again the two groups met on the lip of the chasm and paused to laugh and joke. He was positive that he recognized Howard Hunter's cultured voice saying, "This load and we're finished for tonight. We've got all the mules can pack. Tomorrow night we'll move the stuff out."

The sound of footsteps died away. Slade wondered if he would be able to hold out till the last loads were carried to the cave and the way would be clear for him to escape. He grimly vowed he *would* hold out, and live to even the score for the torture he was undergoing.

With a gasp of dismay, he realized that the shallow shattered ledge which supported his foot was slowly crumbling under his weight; the strain on his arms was increasing. Looked like curtains! But with dogged courage he held on, resisting the urge to let go and get it all over with, to rejoice for an instant in the torment of endurance stretched to the breaking point.

Once again the sound of footsteps. Once again the rumble of voices as the groups met. A wide-swung lantern cast a glare of light over his motionless form. He tensed for the shout of discovery.

It didn't come. The voices began to recede, calling "So long!" "See you tomorrow!"

Breathing unutterable relief, Slade relaxed a trifle, easing his aching muscles. He let go with one hand, flexing the fingers to get some feeling back into them, repeated the action with the other hand. Then he began the slow, laborious climb up the slope, pausing from time to time to rest. Once it appeared he had reached the end of his rope. His feet rested solidly on a ledge of rock, but his groping fingers could find no hold with which he could draw himself up. He tensed his muscles and sprang upward, clutching and clawing. The fingers of his right hand coiled about a fang of stone. A moment of desperate struggle and he got a grip with the other hand. A pause to steady his nerves and he resumed the frightful struggle.

For an eternity of exhausting effort he inched his way up the slope. Finally he got one arm over the lip of the chasm, then the other, then his breast. One last despairing surge that drained away the remaining dregs of his strength and he lay prone on the floor of the cave, drenched with sweat, shaking in every limb.

Gradually his strength returned. He struggled to a sitting position, his back against the wall of the cave and with fingers that still trembled woefully, he managed to roll and light a cigarette, carefully cupping the match in his hands, risking the chance that the tiny flicker would be observed, although he thought there was little likelihood that it would be.

A few deep drags helped a lot. He got to his feet, pinched out the butt and crept down the cave. All was silent and dark as he neared the big rock-walled room, save for the breathing of tethered animals that dulled the sharp edge of the stillness. He struck a match. Its brief flame showed no sign of the outlaws; only the mules remained, and the sacks stuffed with highgrade ore. The match flickered out, the darkness closed in. With long strides, the Ranger hurried down the tunnel to pause under the stars he had at one time never hoped to see again.

Without mishap he gained the thicket that concealed his horse. A few minutes later, Shadow fled up the canyon like a frightened patch of animated midnight.

SIXTEEN

As he rode, Slade conned over the situation in his mind, covering every angle in minutest detail, and finally evolving a plan that he believed to be foolproof. He was deathly tired when he reached the stable and after caring for his horse he tumbled into bed and slept soundly for several hours, awakening greatly refreshed.

Ravenously hungry, he headed for the Branding Pen and something to eat, rejoicing in the bright sunshine of late morning so beautifully in contrast to that cave of horror which had so nearly been his tomb.

Before he finished eating, Carry Farr put in an appearance. Together they repaired to the back room, where Slade regaled the saloonkeeper with an account of the happenings of the tempestuous night before.

"Get the sheriff," he concluded, "and send for John Mosby. Bring them both here and we'll see if we can't set a trap for those coyotes when they crawl out of their hole."

"We'll get 'em!" vowed Farr. "The ornery hydrophobia skunks! What a night you had! It's a wonder your hair ain't as gray as Wes Cole's."

"Maybe it is," Slade chuckled. "I didn't risk looking."

Farr limped out to attend to the chores. Slade sat smoking and thinking, reviewing his plan against any possible flaw, or loophole by which the quarry might escape. Not for a minute did he underestimate Howard Hunter's ability, his genius for detail. He credited Hunter with outstanding perspicacity; the mine owner always looked ahead and took precautions against the unexpected. One slip and he and his posse would be the ones to experience the unpleasant surprise, not the outlaws. He tried in every way to bulwark against that highly undesirable possibility.

One of the reasons for Walt Slade's success as a Ranger was his care never to discount the ability of his opponent, whether in drawing a gun or formulating a plan of action; he gave the other fellow credit for being smart, and endeavored to be just a little smarter, with uniform mastery in that important field. So far, at least. Tonight he hoped to outmaneuver a shrewd and salty bunch, knowing well it would take very little to tip the balance one way or the other. He racked his brains in an endeavor to prepare in advance against any stratagem Hunter might be holding in reserve against just such a contingency as the night would bring forth. He hoped that overconfidence might cloud Hunter's judgment and render him careless, although he was not disposed to count on that possibility; Howard Hunter was hardly the sort to grow careless under any circumstances.

"Well, if I've forgotten something it's liable to be just too bad," he told his cigarette. "Here's hoping I haven't."

He wondered if the canny Hunter might be keeping tabs on the sheriff and Carry Farr and even John Mosby. If so, he might suspect something and go for cover. Slade had warned Farr not to personally conduct Sheriff Cole to the Branding Pen and to send a trusted messenger to summon Mosby and warn him not to make his entrance conspicuous. He believed Mosby and the sheriff would follow instructions and do nothing to arouse the suspicion of any watcher set to observe their movements and report anything that appeared out of the ordinary.

That Hunter kept the Branding Pen under surveillance was obvious; witness the fact that the dead shotgun-wielder who invaded the back room had been seen drinking at the bar but a short time before.

However, Slade relied upon the earliness of the hour to reduce the likelihood of a spy being present at the moment.

One disquieting possibility was that a swamper or some minor kitchen employee might be in cahoots with Hunter. But since the episode of the missing bolt, which could only have been removed by somebody inside the saloon and able to gain access to the back room and work unobserved for a few minutes, Farr had been extremely careful in whom he hired; so that the Ranger was not too much concerned over that angle.

An astounded man was Sheriff Cole when Slade placed the star of the Rangers on the table before him.

"Now I've seen everything," he declared. "El Halcon a Texas Ranger! I'm looking forward to the day when John Wesley Hardin, Sam Bass, King Fisher, Ben Thompson and Curly Bill Brocius will show up and conduct a camp meeting revival."

"Perhaps their ghosts have reformed and will do just that, but I rather doubt that you will see them in the flesh," Slade smiled.

Old John Mosby, on the other hand, didn't appear unduly surprised at the revelation.

"Been wondering for a spell," he said. "You do things like a Ranger, and I know a bit how Jim McNelty works. But what you've showed us about Hunter sure knocks the props from under me. Never would have suspected it; he always seemed such a nice feller."

"In a way he is," Slade conceded. "That is in his everyday association with his fellows. Two sides to him. One which he displays to the public, the other hard as tempered steel and utterly vicious. He's a killer who joys in killing. Murder to him is not just the necessary adjunct to outlaw activities, but a sadistic pleasure. He's in the same category

172

as Gulden, the cannibal, but with more brains. Well, here's hoping he's at the end of his rope.

"And," he added grimly, "I'm confident that he is. Now here's how we'll work it."

Slade paused to carefully marshal his words, and for a last review of every detail of his plan. The others leaned forward expectantly. The hum of talk in the saloon sounded loud in contrast to the utter stillness of the back room. He instinctively glanced at the door, although he knew it was locked, and lowered his voice.

"What we must remember, and continue to remember, is that we are up against an intelligence far above the average," he said slowly. "The brain which conceived and put into execution the scheme for robbing the Comstock mine is that of a mad genius gone wrong. Howard Hunter misses no bets and is usually one jump ahead of the opposition. We don't want that to happen in this instance. Otherwise we may find ourselves in the position of old man Chismy and his cowboys who tried to run down the Cholla Raiders and got blown from under their hats. One little slip on our part and that's right where we'll be."

He paused to note the effect of his words on his hearers. Mosby and the sheriff looked a little uncomfortable, but Carry Farr sat stern and immutable and the grim lines of his ugly face seemed to have deepened. His eyes glowed with fixed purpose.

"Yes, we are going against a hard bunch and a smart one," Slade continued. "It's up to us to be just a little harder and just a little smarter. If somebody gives away what we have in mind, there will be a trap set for us, and no mercy shown. Hunter and his men don't look for any mercy if a showdown comes, and they won't hand out any."

Again he paused, and then addressed the sheriff directly. "Cole, it's up to you to round up and select men who can not only shoot straight and fast but who can be relied upon to keep their mouths shut. No chain is stronger than its weakest link, and if one of those you decide upon should happen to do a little loose talking before we're ready to start, the wrong pair of ears may over-hear it and spoil everything."

"Don't worry about that, I'll get fellers who can be depended on," the sheriff promised grimly. "Fellers who are itching to get a whack at those ornery sidewinders. Men like Chismy and his hands and those two stage guards left good friends behind who'll like nothing better than a chance to even up the score."

Slade nodded. He believed the sheriff and had confidence in his judgment.

"We'll ride down the canyon until we come to the spot where the brush is cut," he concluded. "If we can get there without something happening, we'll hole up and wait for the bunch to show. An hour or two after midnight should be about the time, I figure. Has anybody a suggestion he thinks might better the plan?"

There was silence and a shaking of heads.

"Looks foolproof to me," said Sheriff Cole. The others nodded agreement.

"Should work out, I believe, barring unforeseen accidents," Slade said. "Okay, get going, Cole. Mosby, you know what to do. Carry and I will join you at the last minute. Good hunting."

The meeting broke up. Mosby and the sheriff left by the back door. Slade and Farr sat at the table smoking for a while, then sauntered into the saloon.

"I don't think anybody has caught on," said Farr, running his eye over the sprinkling of customers present at the early hour. "I know all the fellers in here and I'm pretty sure none of them is in cahoots with Hunter."

"I hope not," Slade replied. "Well, all we can do is hope for the best—and do our best. See you later."

Sheriff Cole chose his posse with great care. Men of unquestioned fighting ability and whose reputation for discretion was of the best. After dark, one at a time, the possemen began drifting out of town, some riding one direction, others another, to assemble at the edge of the growth across from the Comstock mine. Shortly after midnight all were on hand. Slade and Carry Farr had left Cholla a little before twelve o'clock, by different routes.

"Think the hellions will come down this way?" the sheriff asked.

"I doubt it," Slade replied. "They have another way of reaching the canyon, through the hills, by which they pack the stolen ore to Hunter's stamp mill. I think they use it more often, for I noticed more footprints coming up the lower canyon over that patch of soft ground than going down. All set? Okay, let's get going. Take your time and keep in the shadow. We're taking no chances of being spotted. That clever devil misses no bets and there's no telling what precautions he takes. We'll try and stay one jump ahead of him, otherwise some of us will stand a good chance to take the Big Jump."

Slade rode at the head of the posse, the sheriff beside him. Following close were Carry Farr and John Mosby. On Slade's broad breast gleamed the star of the Rangers. His face was bleak, his eyes the color of a glacier lake under a stormy sky, and as cold.

"Keep close to the brush," Slade cautioned again. "Moonlight's mighty bright tonight and sharp eyes can see a long ways. Good shooting light, too," he added significantly.

The posse took the hint, and there was no straying from the protecting shadow.

"In the daytime, this hole is always gloomy and

ugly, but in the moonlight, I'm darned if it ain't real purty," Sheriff Cole remarked contemplatively.

Slade nodded agreement. The full glory of the moon was flooding the canyon floor with its white radiance and edging with silver the tall and stiff chaparral. To the south the gorge floor fell away and fell away again to where a mist of gray vapor marked the lower canyon. And beyond, the hills rose tier on tier to the shadowy outline of the mountains further on against the small patches of hurrying clouds and the light-washed sky. Beauty and peace. In stark contrast to the hellish turmoil that might well erupt in a few short hours or less.

Not until they were opposite where the hidden cave mouth waited beyond the screen of growth did Slade draw rein.

"They're not here yet," he announced, gazing across the narrow gorge.

"How do you know?" asked Farr.

"The stand of cut brush is still in place, and they'd hardly replace it after riding into the cave, knowing they'd just have to pull it down again in a short while," Slade explained. "We'll wait here a bit, anyhow. If they're really not here yet, and I don't think they are, they should show very shortly; they'll figure to get the stuff to the stamp mill or wherever they dump it before daylight. Just take it easy, and be ready to grab a horse's nose if he shows signs of singing a song to the stars."

The possemen nodded their understanding and sat their saddles tense and alert.

A full half hour passed before a sound drifted up from the south, a soft, muffled sound that gradually was identified as the clump of horses' hoofs on the earth floor. A group of horsemen materialized from the shadows to draw rein in front of the growth directly opposite from where the posse waited.

"It's them!" Sheriff Cole whispered excitedly. "Shall we jump 'em?"

"What for?" Slade replied in the same guarded tones. "For riding up the canyon? No law against that I ever heard of. No, we must get them dead to rights, which means coming out with the ore. See? They're pulling up the cut brush. Wait till they're all inside before we make a move, and hope they'll all go in."

The horsemen had dismounted and were busily at work. All save one, tall and broad, who remained in the saddle directing operations, the moonlight glinting on his black beard and what appeared to be black hair, but which Slade shrewdly suspected was a black handkerchief bound about his head.

Soon an opening in the growth took form. Into it the riders led their horses, the mounted man following; the darkness of the "tunnel" in the brush swallowed them up. The cut bushes were left stacked beside the opening.

"Okay," Slade whispered. "Leave the horses here with one man to watch them and keep them quiet. Don't forget to bring the flares along, and be ready for business. It's a salty bunch and I doubt if they'll be taken without a fight. If it comes to gunfire, and I think it will, shoot fast and shoot straight. Let's go!"

Slade led the way in the shadow of the brush until they were some distance down the canyon, to where it curved slightly. Then he risked crossing the gorge. It was a nerve-wracking business and a universal sigh of relief was breathed when they reached the opposite stand of growth without hearing the boom of a gun or the whistle of lead.

Then began a slow and tedious crawl north along the edge of the growth with the greatest care to dislodge no loose stone, to snap no twig. They were perhaps a dozen yards from the cut in the brush when Slade suddenly whispered, "Hold it!"

Instantly the posse froze to immobility.

"What is it?" breathed the sheriff.

"Look, right at the edge of the cut," Slade whispered. "There! See that little red spark. There's a jigger standing there smoking a cigarette. When he takes a drag the tip glows. They left a watchman outside to warn them if anybody rides up or down the canyon. He must be gotten out of the way, and without any noise. For very likely there's another one at the cave mouth or just inside it to relay the warning to the rest of the bunch."

"What if he did?" asked the sheriff under his breath. "We'll still have 'em inside, and they couldn't get out."

"Don't be too sure," Slade replied. "Trust Hunter to have a bolt hole somewhere, perhaps by way of the Comstock tunnels. Posting somebody by the brush as a lookout points that way. We've got to get rid of the hellion."

"How?"

Slade stood silent for a moment, and before he framed an answer, the glowing butt of the cigarette described an arc to the ground and a man stepped into view, looking this way and that, and stood leaning on something, very likely a rifle barrel.

"I'll see what I can make of him," Slade breathed. "Stay put and don't make any noise."

Before anybody could protest, he was gliding along in the shadow of the brush, silently as the shadows themselves. The tense watchers strained their eyes to follow him, but he was practically invisible against the dark background of the chaparral.

The sentry turned and started to walk slowly across the opening in the brush. Slade took advantage of his back and glided on a half dozen paces before the man again faced in his direction. He crouched motionless behind a bush and waited.

The sentry sauntered along, humming a little

tune. When he reached the south edge of the cut he halted and leaned his rifle against a convenient twig, removed his hat and scratched his head. He gazed straight at the bush behind which Slade was crouched, and it seemed to strike him that it did not look just right. He replaced his hat, stooped down, picked up a little pebble and threw it at the bush. It struck Slade on the shoulder with a soft plop and rolled to the ground. Had it struck one of his guns or his belt buckle, the clink would surely have betrayed him.

Apparently satisfied that there was nothing wrong, the guard gave over his investigation and, slouching against the brush, stood bathed in a shaft of moonlight, gazing idly at the bush, presumably plunged in a reverie, for he continued to hum softly and his attitude was one of indolent relaxation.

To the watching posse, their nerves strained to the breaking point, it seemed the outlaw stood gazing at that bush for an hour. Really it was less than a minute, although Slade, his muscles aching from his cramped position, would have been inclined to agree with the posse's estimate.

The sentry rubbed his hands together and began to walk forward briskly to warm himself, for the night had turned cool. Doubtless the cold metal of his rifle was unpleasant to the touch, for he left it leaning against the twig. Slade again took advantage of his back to take three long strides forward. Almost at the south edge of the cutting he halted and stood rigid in the deeper shadow as the guard turned. The sweating watchers, who had seen his body flicker for an instant in the moonlight, held their breaths.

Back came the sentry, beating his hands against his thighs and flexing his fingers. He reached the edge of the cutting where the Ranger stood motionless within a yard of him, turned and gazed up the canyon toward where an owl was hooting persistently.

The posse saw Slade make a spring, his hands outstretched toward the watchman's throat. There followed a convulsive twining of the two bodies, the sentry's head bending backward. A sharp crack, something like that of a dry twig snapping, reached the posse's ears and the sentry fell to the ground, his limbs moving spasmodically.

"Good gosh!" gasped the sheriff. "Busted his neck like a match stem! That big jigger don't know his own strength!"

For a moment Slade knelt over his victim, still gripping his throat, then he arose and beckoned the posse to advance.

"That takes care of that," he whispered when his men joined him. "Right here is where we'll make our stand. Have the flares ready to light the instant I call out, not before. Toss them right into the cut. That will give us good shooting light and they won't be able to see us very well, even in the moonlight. Be on your toes. As I said, I don't think they'll be taken without a fight. Shoot straight and shoot fast, and keep on shooting till they're either all down or are yelling 'uncle.' All set? Quiet, now; they should be showing before long. Not very far in to that big cave, and the stuff was all ready to load."

SEVENTEEN

There came a long and tedious wait, the most disagreeable part of a fight, when one grows apprehensive and begins to reflect earnestly upon one's sins. Slade knew his men were growing nervous; it could be told by their sideways glances and the slight shifting of their feet. He himself began to wonder if Howard Hunter had in some miraculous manner divined their presence and was even then leading his outlaws to safety by way of some hidden passage or through the tunnels of the Comstock mine. Would be in keeping with the shrewd hellion's character. He even contemplated entering the cave and attacking the Raiders there. Which, he was forced to admit, would be, under present circumstances and conditions, the act of a stark, staring lunatic. He resolutely put the thought behind him and resigned himself to patience.

All things come to him who waits, and sometimes to him who doesn't. And eventually the outlaws came to Slade and his posse. From beyond the dark passage through the brush sounded a faint clicking that steadily loudened, the beat of shod hoofs on the stone floor of the cave.

There followed a rustling and crackling, as if some large object were being forced through the narrow lane in the brush. Another moment and a weirdly distorted shape bulged into the moonlight. Another and another. They were mules bearing huge aparejos or packsaddles. A full half dozen of them. Next came a group of men on foot. Slade counted seven altogether. Again the clicking of hoofs and two horsemen rode into view. The men on foot began replacing the cut brush, wedging the stake ends of the trunks deep in the ground.

"Flares ready!" Slade whispered. Another instant and the oil soaked torches flared with a roar and were tossed to the edge of the brush. Slade's voice rang out:

"In the name of the State of Texas! You are under arrest! Anything you say may be used against you! Get your hands up, you're covered!"

The blazing flares revealed the outlaws frozen in grotesque attitudes. They also dimly showed the grim possemen, cocked rifles to their shoulders, eyes glinting back of the sights.

There was a crawling second of paralyzed inaction. Then the gun in the hand of one of the horsemen blazed. A posseman went down with a queer little grunt.

Instantly the leveled rifles flamed and roared. Outlaws fell like grain before a reaper's sickle. There was a wild scattering, a spiteful crackle of six-guns, then yells for mercy.

Crashing from the milling group burst the two horsemen, speeding up the canyon, the posse's bullets whining after them. But they kept going, faster by the second.

Walt Slade raced across the canyon, whistling a loud, clear note. There was an answering snort and Shadow surged to meet him. Slade swung into the saddle with the black horse still in motion. He settled his feet in the stirrups, gathered up the split reins. His voice rang out again:

"Trail, Shadow! Trail!"

With a plunge the great horse shot forward, his irons drumming the hard soil, his mane rippling in the wind of his passing. He snorted, slugged his head above the bit and literally poured his long body over the ground. Slade, swaying easily in the saddle, kept his eyes fixed on the two fugitives, now far ahead.

"They can't turn off anywhere," he told Shadow. "And if they think they can run away from you, feller, they've got another guess coming."

Shadow snorted agreement and redoubled his efforts.

Quickly Slade saw that one of the fleeing riders was falling behind his companion, who was superbly mounted. Shadow, fleeting through the pale moonlight, was steadily overhauling him. From time to time the rider turned to glance back at his pursuer, his face a white blob in the moonglow. He was now less than three hundred yards to the front, and the three hundred slowly shrank to little more than half that distance.

The fugitive gave up trying to outdistance the black horse. He jerked his mount to a slithering halt, whirled him around. Slade saw the glint of shifted metal and swung far to one side, drawing his Winchester from the boot as he did so.

Flame gushed through the moonlight; Slade heard the whine of the passing slug.

"Easy, Shadow, easy!" he called, and clamped the Winchester to his shoulder.

Instantly Shadow leveled off to a smooth running walk. Another bullet whispered in Slade's ear. Then his own rifle bucked against his shoulder.

Shot after shot he fired, swiftly as he could work the ejection lever. He saw the horseman reel, try to steady himself, lean slowly sideways and fall to lie on his back, arms widespread. The riderless horse dashed away across the canyon.

Walt Slade, thundering past, leaned far over to glance at the dead face of Park Crony, the giant foreman of Howard Hunter's Last Nugget mine.

The other fugitive had gained a little and was crashing on toward the distant north mouth of the canyon, leaning low in the saddle, urging a splendid dark bay horse to do its utmost.

The bay was giving his all, but it was not enough. Slowly, slowly, Shadow closed the distance. The moonlight glinted on the rider's black beard as he turned his head to glance back.

"The big skookum he-wolf of the pack, horse," Slade told Shadow. "Sift sand, we'll get him!"

Soon the bay's rider was within pistol range, but Slade held his fire, hoping to get in a shot that would only wound. The light was strengthening as the dawn painted the east with rosy fingers. The stars grew pale and paler, changed from gold to silver, to needle points of steel pricking the blue-black velvet of the sky. The moon waxed wan and her mountain ridges stood out clear against her sickly face like the bones on the face of a dying man. The hill crests were bathed in a tremulous golden glow.

And still the two gallant horses raced on with unabated speed, with Shadow slowly but surely gaining. Slade reached for his gun butt, steadied the black horse. Then with unexpected suddenness the end came.

Like a shot rabbit, the big bay went end over end, hurling his rider from the saddle like a stone from a sling. Horse and man crashed through the brush, rolled over and over and lay still.

"Put his foot in a badger hole!" Slade exclaimed as Shadow hurtled forward. Before the tall black came to a plunging halt Slade was out of the saddle. His feet touched the ground as the bay's rider surged erect, hand flickering to his gun with a speed like to the beat of a bird's wing.

It was oily-smooth perfection, that draw, and blinding fast, but Slade's Colt boomed a breath-second before smoke wisped from the bearded man's gun.

Slade felt the stinging burn of a bullet flicking the skin of his cheek, but he stood sternly erect, holding his fire as the bearded man reeled back, let his gun fall from a nerveless hand and slowly sank to the ground.

Holstering his gun, Slade knelt beside him, gazing into the already dimming blue eyes. He gripped the black beard with deft fingers, gently slipped the hooks that held it in place from over the dying man's ears to reveal the pain-distorted but still strangely handsome face of Howard Hunter. He began unbuttoning Hunter's shirt, the front of which was drenched with blood.

Hunter was nearly unconscious, but he rallied a little at Slade's touch.

"You can't do anything," he gasped. "Filling up inside. Artery or big vein cut. Soon be over, and I don't much care. So you're a Ranger! Might have known it. Thought you were just another owlhoot trying to horn in, like a bunch from over New Mexico way did a while back. We took care of them, in the Cattlemen's Club. Tried to take care of you. Didn't work. If I'd known you were a Ranger I wouldn't have tried. Made up my mind to quit when the Rangers showed up. About ready to quit and go straight, anyhow. Can't straighten a crooked trail, Ranger, can't straighten a crooked trail!"

The ghost of a smile flitted over the dying man's face. For a moment he was silent, apparently summoning what little strength he had left for a last effort. He spoke again:

"Was a mining engineer and a good one. Got sucked into a shady deal, up in Nevada. Lost my job. Wife left me. Hated the world and everybody in it. Wanted to get even. Got mixed up with a bad crowd. More trouble. That's how I learned to handle burglar's tools. Came south and took up prospecting. Figured then to go straight. Mosby striking the Comstock after I made the mistake of taking the wrong trail set me off again. Hated everybody. Figured to get even. Got an outfit of my old pals together and organized the Cholla Raiders. Found that cave when I was prospecting the canyon trying to hit on another Comstock. Triangulated the route it took and the distance and knew it must run mighty close to the Comstock tunnels. It did. Had to pull robberies to get quick money for my bunch. Real money was coming from the highgrade ore. Yes, I figured to go straight. Enough money stashed away in the mine office safe to put me on easy street. But you can't . . . straighten . . . a . . . crooked . . . trail!"

Hunter's voice had been growing weaker and weaker. Once again he smiled, a wan, fleeting smile. He sank back, his blue eyes fixed and cold.

Walt Slade stood up and gazed down at the dead face; his own eyes were sad. Why, he wondered did one of such outstanding ability have to take the wrong fork in the road? Mounting his horse he

190

rode back down canyon through the glory of the morning, to where the sheriff and his posse waited with their prisoners and their dead.

"Get 'em both?" Cole asked.

Slade nodded. He did not want to talk about it. The sheriff, after a searching glance, refrained from asking for details.

"Some Comstock muckers and rock busters mixed up in the ore stealing, the prisoners told us," he said, jerking his head toward the cave. "Park Crony had them under his thumb. They didn't have anything to do with the robberies and killings. Didn't even know Hunter was mixed up in them. The prisoners gave me their names."

"Round them up and give them a good lecture and chase them out of the section," Slade advised. "Just hired hands out to make a crooked dollar. Not worth the expense of keeping them in jail. Well, suppose we get back to town. My chore here is finished and after something to eat and some sleep, I'll be riding. The chances are Captain Jim will have another little chore lined up for me by the time I get back to the Post."

Just as the sun was setting in golden flame, they watched him ride away, laughter and anticipation in his eyes, to where duty called and danger and new adventure waited.

"He rides to tomorrow," murmured Miguel, the little guitarist. "May for him the dawn be always bright!"

Center Point Large Print
600 Brooks Road / PO Box 1
Thorndike, ME 04986-0001 USA

(207) 568-3717

US & Canada:
1 800 929-9108
www.centerpointlargeprint.com